Unfinished Stories of Girls

Unfinished Stories of Girls

Catherine Zobal Dent

Fomite
Burlington, VT

Stories from this collection have appeared in the following publications. The author expresses her gratitude to the supportive editors of: *Crab Orchard Review, Drunken Boat, EAPSU, echolocation, Elsewhere: A Literature of Place, Harvard Review, Louisville Review, The MacGuffin, PANK, Paterson Literary Review*, and *Portland Review.*

ISBN-13: 978-1-937677-62-6
Library of Congress Control Number: 2013952786

Fomite
58 Peru Street
Burlington, VT 05401
www.fomitepress.com

For my brothers
George, Robert, and Johnny
CZD

For my mother, Nancy
AP

CONTENTS

The mothers have beautiful old lady legs.
The silence in them spills into us,
we are as shhhh as we can be.

—CATHERINE BARNETT
The Game of Boxes

At the Mouth

AT THE END OF A LONG OYSTERSHELL LANE, there once was a girl named Ella Robinson who lived with her grandmother. Their lane came out near a godforsaken public boat ramp called Covey's Landing, where I grew up fishing and hunting with my uncles and father. You could be fined a hundred-fifty dollars for littering at Covey's Landing, the county sign said, but kids tossed beer cans and condoms into the honeysuckle, and other people threw snarled lines and sun-cracked drink holders and empty bait cups on the pavement, and hunters left Skoal cans and shotgun shells and magazines with torn pictures of deer. But off the landing, the Tuckahoe River coiled by, tidal and beautiful, and after her grandmother died, Ella Robinson would stand at the river among the cigarette butts and shards of glass, like a heron looking over the water. That's how she approached all the men.

I'm not telling which one I am.

Ella talked all the time. She was like a lonely fishing net I got caught up in. Once, she told me how on her last day of high school she came home to find her grandmother's body on the kitchen floor, her poor grandmother's eyes bulging like a crab's. Ella called 911, and the ambulance driver said Grandmother had choked on her tongue. "Poor woman," he said, Ella told me with a weird look. Other men got out, but not me, not all the time. I listened to how Ella went to graduation alone and sat in her quiet house afterward and remembered the husky ambulance man saying, *Poor woman, poor woman,* and I listened to how the next day she drove her grandmother's pickup truck back to Easton High, where the teachers were boxing up for summer, and Ella asked for help casting her body in plaster. I think the art teacher saw herself in Ella, that's why she said yes, why she helped Ella make a full-scale copy of herself, kneeling, hand to mouth, as if covering a yawn.

Once both halves were cast, and the plaster dried, and the mould chipped away, Ella drove herself home in the truck bed. She set her figure on the kitchen floor over butcher paper to catch the spills. One palm, two knees, and ten toes, she painted green with a round brush, Ella told me, and she painted hydrangea blossoms on the breasts, and cornflowers over each eye, and hollyhocks going up the thighs, and a pink hibiscus on the crotch.

I can see her pausing and biting her thumbnail, looking at her statue, listening to a long-legged wasp bump at the window screen, thinking how everything was trying to get inside.

People around here remember the time a kid's yellow Labrador jumped after a stick and disappeared into the Tuckahoe, a whorl, water-flattened fur and tawny head, then nothing, as if the dog shouldn't have existed in the first place. Hunters swear they've seen pintail ducks struggle to keep their balance, and fishermen warn that it's easier to skin a catfish than row against the current. Farmers say the river sucks down tree branches as big as a man's wrist.

Ella's knees, double-jointed like the rest of her, warped back when she stood on the edge of the Tuckahoe. She used to stare into the water, and I used to stare at her. Ever since she was a little kid, she'd looked almost the same, with a star-shaped scar on her temple where she'd been bitten by a dog. Her crooked, yellowish face narrowed to a point like a branch. She had full breasts, low hips, a protruding bellybutton. God, I loved that girl's legs, how they hard-locked into curves. Her period had come when she was twelve, and she often talked about it. She imitated her grandmother, snapping, "Why'd it have to happen just like your mother?" Her grandmother quoted scripture from the Bible, her gray braid wrapping her head like a halo. Ella quoted her grandmother. "If a man lies with a woman during her menstrual period," they both said, "the two shall be cut off from their people, for they have laid bare the flowing fountain of blood." People around here didn't really keep up with old Grandmother Robinson, but we all knew she saw things that didn't exist, like invisible cats, and mice the cats caught, which she carried out the door by invisible tails. The farmer who managed her fields says Mrs. Robinson saw Jesus and the saints, and sometimes forgot her granddaughter's name.

Hidden from the road by trees, the one-story Robinson house contained a living room with an old upright piano and a wooden crucifix, a tiny mint-green kitchen, two bedrooms, and a shallow, concrete basement. A raised porch surveyed the lawn, and the siding dropped into deep, dry, window wells. In her grandmother's chest of drawers, Ella found a crocheted doily which she glued on the crown of her naked statue. She moved it onto the porch, and she would rest there, just listening, alone.

Two weeks after her grandmother died, Ella, on the porch beside her statue, heard a noise, a furtive rustle. A snapping turtle had fallen in the window well and was burying itself in stones and dry leaves. Ella told me how she tried to rescue it with a shovel. The turtle struck at her hand, at the metal head of the shovel, and at the hard well walls. It was simpleminded and too heavy to lift, so eventually she left it alone. That night, she sank into a bath lit by candles from under her grandmother's bed and saw something that didn't exist: her grandmother, dead Grandmother, floating above the water like a mirror.

"Pookin," the specter called with a deep voice, "do not fear those who kill the body, that's Matthew 10:28."

The clock on the bathroom shelf reflected the moon hovering in the sky. Ella, when she told me about it, remembered her hands opening like smooth buds into palms. She put her palms over her ears but couldn't keep out Grandmother's words.

"The Lord's voice shakes the oaks and strips the leaves, Pookin. Go down to the landing and collect the trash."

So Ella, wrapped in a bathrobe, went outside, past her replica on the porch and past the turtle in its cell-like nest. Light as a cat, she strode over the oyster shell lane and turned down the road toward Covey's Landing, her hands glowing white on the ends of her arms, her sneakers shining from the bottom of her robe. She'd thought the public landing would be busy with kids smoking cigarettes on car hoods and necking in back seats, but to her surprise, there were no parties, no teens, just weeping willow branches curled together in the mud. Ella told me she didn't know what to do so she picked up an empty beer bottle and filled it with cigarette butts. Back home she set the bottle and a pair of discarded underpants and a crushed Budweiser can on the porch by her painted self. She washed her hands with Grandmother's sage-scented soap and lay down in Grandmother's bed.

I can imagine her there in the half-dark, pensive, all alone.

ELLA TOLD ME that once, when she was twelve, with her period and new breasts, she and Grandmother had paged through a graphic booklet on sex. Grandmother had *Oh'd* over the pictures and covered her mouth with her knuckles. She told Ella that people did awful things despite God's law, that Ella better not try such sinful stuff. Grandmother went into her room and made phone calls, and Ella heard screaming. That night as they ate beaten biscuits and gravy, some people arrived from Dorchester General Hospital to take Grandmother away. Ella hid in the cupboard. She rode the school bus in the morning. That afternoon, there was still no Grandmother, so she heated up leftovers in the oven. In the middle of her meal, the kitchen door opened, and there stood Grandmother, saying, "A dog goes back to what it's vomited, Proverbs 26:11." Ella told me about the naked pictures and dog vomit and gravy and said that she didn't know where the sex booklet had come from, but she knew it ended up in the trash.

After the night of the bath and candle shadows, Grandmother came often to visit Ella, sending her again and again to the landing.

The instructions came late over the screeching of crickets in the sumac and cicadas in the willow trees. That was before she had started talking to me, or any of the men. She would walk down the country road in the dark, her legs like sandhill cranes, like stalks of muscle and blood. She was the limbs of God. She collected the trash and brought it back to her house in thin white grocery bags that mounded up on the porch next to the naked statue and in the living room and on Ella's twin bed. No one came to visit except the farmer who worked the fields, telling Ella he was watching out for her. Because her house smelled of beer drippings and wet socks, the farmer made her uneasy, and she kept him on the porch where he stared at the statue, hand up to its mouth as if bored or perhaps surprised.

Ella told me that one night down at the landing she was thinking of the turtle that didn't rustle anymore in the window well. In the midst of her thoughts, Grandmother appeared on the water, twirling a finger in her long gray hair. "Divided tongues like tongues of fire fell on the disciples' heads and they could speak in wild languages," she said.

"That snapping turtle," Ella told me she asked, "did it walk up from the river to lay eggs?"

"At the willow I will comfort you with flagons," Grandmother said, "but first, get rid of false idols."

It was hard to interpret, Ella never had understood scripture, but the next morning, she heaped all the bags on the porch around her statue. In broad daylight, she walked to the landing where Grandmother showed her the first man. He was hip-high in the river, stringing decoys, wooden ducks that stretched in a line like a waning moon. At the sight, Grandmother whispered, "The day of the Lord will come like a thief."

Ella waded into the water, not sure what to do next. She opened her mouth and said, "Will you follow me?"

Back in Grandmother's bed, she traced three inky serpents tattooed on the man's shoulder. He was a white middle-aged trucker of fuel oil. His wife owned Glenda's Wild Den of Tanning on Goldsborough Street, and he told Ella that he fished every weekend while his wife ran the booths for naked women. Ella lifted her head, eyes open, and looked at the ceiling. She murmured, "Oh, Pookin."

The trucker laughed. "What the heck?"

"That's what Grandmother calls me." She opened her mouth like a cat, licked his arm, and lost her virginity to him, quickly, with a little blood but no fuss. As he pulled back on his cowboy boots, she asked if he knew anything about turtles, or fountains, or flagons.

"Girl, what the heck are you about?"

"Will you bring me a picture?" Ella asked. "So I can see you when you're not here?"

"Like a dried-up spring," Grandmother intoned. "A cloud blown along by storms."

The second man, a dark-skinned sales agent at Radio Shack, parked at Covey's Landing to mull over how he hated his job. He smelled like furniture polish, Ella told me. He carried condoms in his wallet and liked to kiss and not talk. She pinched the elastic bubble on the tip of the condom, tiny and translucent like spit. Hoping he might show a little curiosity, she shared a few of Grandmother's lines. "The voice of the Lord breaks cedars," she said.

The salesman didn't reply, he just breathed lemony hot in her ear. While lying on top of him like a tarp, Ella asked if he'd bring her a photograph of himself, and he nodded.

"Two bear record in heaven," Grandmother said. "God is love."

The third man, short and squat, sank his teeth into Ella's neck and held on like a puppy. He went to Chesapeake Community College, worked at the Pizza Hut, and still lived with his mother. He bit down steadfastly, like a pit bull, and she liked feeling his lips on her neck. "I am the rose of Sharon," she said to him, "and the lily of the valley."

The young man said, "Huh."

She wanted to see his face but he kept it buried in her hair. The headboard bobbed inches in front of her mouth. "God," she said in intervals to the wall as he pumped. "God, God, God."

She waited for him to revive, but when he came to his senses, he buttoned his pants and was gone.

PEOPLE AROUND HERE know that each of Ella's lovers brought her a picture which she kept in a sequined box. That's what the police told us. They don't know how often Ella washed the sheets on her grandmother's bed, or how she sometimes brought the naked statue in from the porch to kneel beneath the crucifix, or that she'd started calling the statue Saint Evangeline. The trucker had sex with Ella on the floor next to the naked statue, and so did the salesman, and the young guy, and who knows how many of us, gulping like catfish on the shag rug.

ONE NIGHT in late August, Ella went down to the landing. I'd taken to checking up on her pretty often, although I don't think she ever knew I was there. It had been three months since her grandmother's death, and she sat on the edge of the boat ramp, staring at the marsh lilies. The dark summer air rolled up the river in currents, and mosquitoes hummed an erotic tune. Out of the night, a sharp, deep voice rang. It said, "False prophets act by instinct."

It was all I could do not to jump off the ground.

Ella's own voice said, "My blood has stopped, Grandmother."

"Animals born to be captured and killed," the deep voice snapped. "Why is there so much trash?"

Ella rose in the liquid night, the willow fingering her neck. She strode up the lane, and I followed. Her voice, singing, "For I am sick, si-ick, si-i-ick of love," pulled me along. On the porch, she knelt and rummaged among the bags of trash, as if imaginary animals swirled around her ankles, and then she went inside to lie beneath her statue on the living room floor. It was quiet as I crouched on the porch, peering inside. Saint Evangeline's pale fingers stuck to her painted lips. The piano watched over them, and so did Jesus on the crucifix. Through a screen window I saw Ella twitch in her sleep, and late, late that night, I heard more.

"Why didn't you plant a rusty nail to keep our hydrangeas blue?"

"You can talk?" Ella whispered at the statue.

"Why not?" I heard a low voice say.

"But you're not real."

"A turtle lays eggs in sand." The Saint's tone was all fact and reason. She said, "Talk to your lovers. A baby can't grow in a well." Ella fell back asleep then, but Saint Evangeline hovered, persuasive, vindictive, staring at me from her wide, flower eyes.

Ella broached the subject of her pregnancy with all of us. She told me how the married man cursed during sex, but how otherwise he was good and kind. "Pookin," she said quietly to the ceiling one day as he lay beside her, "we forgot about the eggs." She lifted the back of her head from the pillow and stared at a vein riding his forehead. He sucked the skin around her swollen nipple, his mouth a shovel. She handed him a condom.

"Where the heck you get that?" he said. "I always pull out in time."

Of her lovers, Ella told me she most enjoyed kissing the salesman. "The Lord makes me swell," she said the next time he arrived. He put on a condom and lifted her off the bed, clutching her buttocks. A mouth can be hard like metal, or soft like a belly. His sad lips pressed her mouth like tangerines, and she couldn't say anything more.

She told me that the young one cried out in bed one day, "God!"

"I love you," Ella said. She flipped over to catch his eye. "Listen, my blood's stopped. Do you—"

"Uh-uh," he yipped, lips curled.

Grandmother looked up cross-eyed from the sheets. "He who doesn't listen is deafened by ignorance. There's a place reserved in the deepest darkness."

Ella closed her eyes, and so did I, and we all kept coming. It was exciting, it was insane. Pretending to be a cat or a weeping willow, that girl lowered herself onto us in the middle of the bed, wincing at the entry and the union of parts.

She always asked if I felt something, and I never asked what that meant.

LATE IN SEPTEMBER, the cornflowers rose buoyantly from the soybeans. It was a dry Indian summer, and in the window well, the snapping turtle's body had shrunken from its shell. One day when Ella nudged the carcass, its tail fell off. She carried the shell onto the porch and covered it with a plastic grocery bag. Then she sat among the trash bags, and I showed up, and she told me she'd been down to Covey's Landing that morning. It had been busy with men fishing, she said, and country music rolling out of a truck radio, and an old woman licking beer from her cup. A pigtailed girl in underwear had slid off a lap onto a lawn chair, and a golden Labrador had sniffed Ella's hands. She told me that Grandmother glared from behind the trees, waving her arms, saying, "No one knows the day, nor the hour!"

Ella sang to me, "It's all going to work out fine." I shouldn't have listened to the words, I should have kept my hands to myself, but she pulled me close, and she was a crazy hymn. Afterward, I said goodbye, but a few miles down the road, something made me turn back. It was dusk, and I hid behind the warm hydrangeas and let my eyes follow her around as she put trash bags shaped like Easter lilies in the back of the pickup. She carried out the snapping turtle wrapped in plastic, and Saint Evangeline. No one else came to her house that night. I poked around, creeping to the windows, lying on the porch until long after midnight.

I must have fallen asleep because somehow Ella got out without my seeing her. She started the pickup, and I jumped, and climbed in my own car, and left the headlights off. Down at the landing, stars hung overhead in lines like laundry. She stopped, and I stopped, and I snuck down to where she knelt, to hear what she spoke in the night.

"A pig that's been washed goes back to roll in the mud, that's 2 Peter 2:22."

That awful voice, Grandmother's voice, hung over the water. There was a lot of silence, followed by more talking, and more silence. I sat down to see what would happen. I waited, but I fell asleep again, more than once. Just before dawn, I awoke to hear a voice say, "You'll need to tie the plastic tight."

The eastern sky was yellowing. Ella, her face moist like a hibiscus blossom, perched beneath the tissue paper moon.

"Farewell," she called sadly, but I was half asleep, I didn't understand. Saint Evangeline sat on the dark bank watching the mission. By the time I saw Ella in the river, I was too muddled to move, and then I did, and it was too late. The Tuckahoe swept and spiraled. The girl was a snapping turtle on a branch over the river, then a branch slipping into the flow. A loose decoy turned sideways on the surface, and under the surface, a plastic bottle, mouth swallowing the tide. Some early morning fishermen skimmed by, standing on their johnboat, pointing at the figure on the landing, headed for the marsh, surrounded by hundreds of white bags, a human figure crawling like a dog but with a hand up to its mouth. They revved their motor and drew nearer. "Jesus Christ," said one.

People around here tell the story of how they thudded into the body. Pulled her out onto a bank of mud. Untied the bag from her neck. People are still wondering about the statue on the riverbank and the turtle shell, wondering why she left them there. I stayed hidden, and I stay hidden still. Should I have saved Ella from unholy destruction? She did not mean nothing to me, after all. Was it my job, or is it yours?

WHEELS

REBECCA WOULD ALWAYS REMEMBER the moment right before she hit the girl: the cold rush that flooded her face from the truck's air conditioner. The taste of her last cigarette. Steve Miller singing *Time keeps on slippingslippingslipping,* her truck's brakes and tires like a man's scream, and then training wheels lifting off the road, and the girl's eyes, dark pupils circled by white. Afterward Rebecca didn't get out of the driver's seat of her cherry-red Ford pick-up but instead put it in reverse, backed up, and drove on. Rebecca's father Dr. John Sperry would later have to explain to his Dorchester General colleagues how it was that his daughter did not tell anyone right away. How at eighteen it was normal that this kind of trauma would induce shock and how upon recovery Rebecca's good morals led her to do the right thing. On Saturday, May 26, he and Rebecca went together to Officer Bob Swann's office to report her role in the previous day's tragedy.

Our town Cambridge, in tidewater Maryland, was a town much like the surrounding ones. For a twenty mile radius of country clubs and waterside farms, every white person knew every other white

person's name. You could count many of the black citizens into
that circle as well. People also knew the car you drove, your religion, your father's business, your past boyfriend or girlfriend compared with the one you'd wanted, and whether you lived on one of
the beautiful brackish rivers whose tides gave the region its name,
or in town, or in the flat farm fields. Dr. Sperry was Dorchester
General's top cardiologist, a man to be reckoned with. He'd lost
his wife Ann at an early age and so had dated half the nurses at
Dorchester General Hospital. None of us blamed him. He was
devoutly Catholic. In golf, he could occasionally hit a hole-in-one.

Rebecca played on the North Cambridge High lacrosse team and
volunteered weekends with Habitat for Humanity. Like most kids,
she drank but didn't let it get out of hand, and she was someone we
could count on. One time, she drank peach wine coolers and pissed
in Nancy Friend's shower stall and then puked peach vomit on the
pillows, and after that, she drank beer instead. Among beers, she
preferred the red ale brewed by Jenna Williams and her brother and
their friends. She liked playing ping-pong and quarters. Headed to
college, was it Davidson, or Duke? Anyway the same place her
father had gone, a good school, somewhere down south.

When our town learned about the accident, the accidental death
of the little black girl (when we read in the *Star-Republican* that
the grieving family lived in one of the small houses near the Black
Dog Alley trailer park outlying the town of Easton; when we saw
in the obituary that the girl was Eliza Green, a second-grade student at Easton Elementary who "liked to jump rope and write";
when we heard from our neighbor that the deceased girl's father
worked at the Route 50 Jiffy Lube, the nice black man who cleaned

your windows for free and who said, "Drive safe now, ma'am"), many of us experienced conflicting thoughts. The teenager driving was the heart doctor's daughter, the Sperry girl. Never been in trouble before, good girl, headed for college, a degree in medicine, or maybe law, certainly a bright future. Why had the little black girl been riding her bicycle on the road at dusk? Why hadn't the girl's nearby father put a stop to this unsafe game? Where, for God's sake, was the mother? Poor little girl, only seven, riding her bike at dusk on a back road. No one asked where, her truck hurtling so recklessly, Rebecca Sperry had been going, or from where she'd come. No one in our community asked this, no, and least of all Marvin Ewing, the social studies teacher who'd recommended Rebecca for the Citizen's Award she was scheduled to receive one and a half weeks later at North Cambridge High's graduation.

Marvin's student had not yet been told about the award, and he knew for sure that she would be thrilled. Rebecca Sperry was a girl who would go far because she knew how to write a good paper, and she smiled a lot. That time Rebecca had turned in Mindy Wright, not her close friend, but one of her peers, for cheating on Marvin Ewing's Problems of Democracy mid-term, had proven her good judgment, and when Marvin told Rebecca that he would talk to the cheater, but that Rebecca should let it go because Mindy Wright needed a break, forgiveness even, well, Rebecca had been willing to accept his judgment as the right thing. Despite her grade being lower than the cheating girl's. That was compassion in a young person. That was generosity. Monday morning at school in the teacher's lounge before the first bell, when Marvin heard about the accident, he thought there must have been a mistake.

He'd asked, "Why the long faces, folks?"

"Didn't you hear?" Ina Fellows said to Marvin. She set her mug down carefully on the counter and raised her formidable eyebrows. Over at the coffee machine Marvin stopped whistling Dixies Land and stared back at his colleague. How Ina Fellows must turn kids off with those arching brows, those puckered old English-teacher lips. "Rebecca Sperry was involved in a hit and run Friday afternoon. A seven-year-old riding a tricycle."

"My God," Marvin said.

"Wasn't a tricycle, Ina," said Cathy Phelps, the ninth-grade history teacher. "It was a small bike with training wheels."

Ina continued, "Rebecca turned herself in the next day."

"Well, that was good," Marvin said.

Everyone took a moment to think about that.

Marvin asked, "Is anyone pressing charges?"

"The accident was at six o'clock," said the secretary, Mrs. Thornton, poking her gray head in the door to look for someone who was not in the lounge. "It was still light outside."

Cathy Phelps, pragmatic from teaching so much history, said, "I'm sure the dead girl's family doesn't have a lot of money."

In homeroom, the social studies teacher Marvin Ewing saw Gabriel Brooks with his head down on his desk. Nancy Friend's chair was empty. Jenna Williams and Brice Hart leaned on each other, eyes red. Stupid kids, Marvin thought, don't know how good they have it. Cars when they're sixteen, college paid for, only thing they have to worry about is not failing, not getting pregnant, keeping their little stashes of pot low-key, and not getting caught driving drunk. Rebecca would come out of this fine. It had been an accident.

Gabe Brooks fully expected to be pulled out of class that day, but no one ever came to question him.

The dead girl's father Jeb Green would live on from that time in a haze of grief and fury and fury-induced insomnia. He had heard the pick-up truck's purr ever since the four-stop-sign crossing where Black Dog Alley met Covey's Landing Road, but he hadn't said anything to his daughter out near the end of the driveway trying her little sister's training wheels. He was thinking of the problem of the garden hose. How, left running overnight, old rubber develops leaks. Water from the green tube sprayed in seventeen different directions, sprinkling both his temple and his pant cuff. He would have to buy a new hose. He thought about how people were constantly letting you down in ways both important and small. (From that day forward, Jeb would never buy another hose. In fact, he would leave all of the yard and household chores to his wife, Shante Gibbs Green, who'd seen the accident from the kitchen window.)

Social studies teacher Marvin Ewing, that Monday and forever afterward, would not think about how he'd once confiscated a fake ID from Rebecca Sperry, a license that had belonged to Kitty Bailey, a blond former lacrosse player whose father taught math at Green Marsh Middle School, and who by now was in medical school in California. Marvin would think instead how, since that accident had happened at six o'clock in the evening, well then, lucky it was too early for Rebecca to have been drinking. Much. When Marvin Ewing had confiscated the fake I.D. in history class, he told Rebecca that he could turn her in to Dr. Cunningham but believed she had learned an important lesson: You always get caught. Better not get a new I.D., he'd joked. She'd smiled, "You're right, Mr. Ewing."

Father Brian Matthews of Saint Andrew's Church where on Sundays John Sperry, and Ann Sperry too, before her death, had brought Rebecca every weekend since she was born, did not want to consider too hard what he'd heard in confidence from Dr. Cunningham, the principal of North Cambridge High. None of us wanted to consider this. Dr. Cunningham had confessed to Father Matthews what we all knew: Senior Bash, a tradition that had been going on at North Cambridge High since before this generation's grandparents graduated, had been held that Friday. Drawing on memories of his own high school days, Father Matthews had consoled the principal, "No, these are some pretty good kids."

Marvin Ewing wouldn't want to think about how the kids had gotten their alcohol. Ina Fellows wouldn't want to ask how much money Dr. Sperry paid attorney Lucinda Taylor, whose mother was from Cambridge, to come down from Annapolis for his daughter's defense. Cathy Phelps, the pragmatist, would not want to wonder who'd let the girl drive home, who'd seen her leaving Senior Bash and waved, "Later, Rebecca." None of us wanted to think about who swore to the police that yes, while Rebecca Sperry was at Mindy Wright's party, she'd only had one beer tops, and that her one beer had certainly come early in the day, around noon, right when she'd arrived at Senior Bash.

That day, Mindy Wright had hosted Senior Bash up outside Easton, towards Saint Michaels, because her mother owned an estate there on the Miles River. They could use the property and the boats. (Mindy's mom wasn't asking questions, *winkwink*). Gabe Brooks and Nancy Friend and Rebecca Sperry had been partying since noon along with the dozens of others who hooked school that day. When the girls said they were hungry, Gabriel drove them out to the 7-11 on Glebe Road where they bought chilidogs and Slushees and Camel Lights, Gabe and Nancy giggling at the Hindu behind the counter who couldn't seem to count their change. Nancy would later remember but not want to think about how Rebecca, studying the rack of candy, had seemed confused, or how on the parking lot she'd tried to light her cigarette on the wrong end.

"What's wrong with you?" Nancy said.

"It was my idea to come buy cigarettes, what are you talking about?" Rebecca said. The consonants of her words folded in on themselves, but the judgment of Gabe and Nancy, who had each done several shots of tequila, salt on the hand, piece of lime, sitting in Mindy Wright's mother's Jacuzzi, was not sharp. Gabe lit Rebecca's cigarette for her. He'd had a crush on her since eighth grade.

It was dusk when Rebecca tried to brake the truck. Neither Gabriel nor Nancy wanted to think of the thud. No one, not Gabriel nor Nancy (nor the teacher Marvin Ewing nor Dr. Sperry nor anyone), wanted to imagine a rush of metal and rubber and red and limb.

When the obituary came out, the secretary Mrs. Thornton observed aloud to Dr. Cunningham, "It says the little girl liked to write?"

Ray Hatfield, the teacher from Green Marsh Middle who directed plays at both middle and high school, happened to be standing at the copy machine. "My wife's cousin teaches at Easton Elementary," he said. "The girl's teacher, Ruth Callahan, told her the little girl loved to write."

Couldn't trust anyone to do anything in this family, Jeb Green was thinking as he duct-taped that hose. Not shop for groceries, because you had to be careful, so careful to check for rot at the base of the cauliflower, to avoid the dented cans of soup, to inspect the expiration date on the milk. And you couldn't trust anyone else to bring home the money, because you had to be sure the boss treated you fairly, this was a white man's world, and if you wanted to work as a secretary at Bishop Office Supply, or an Agway check-out clerk, well, you were asking for it. Like Shante had with her last two bosses. Better they live on just one salary, Shante looking after the house and the girls. Someone needed to watch after Toni who was five and Eliza who despite her airs was only seven.

Eliza, riding Toni's bike with the training wheels, barely remembered what it was like to be only five.

At seven she felt the power of having learned not only to print and read and do math, but also to write in a secret language, swirled letters called *cursive* that made you never have to pick up your pencil. It was so much fun to connect the words, to loop together a line from a song like *Wheelsonabusgoroundandround*. Miss Callahan, with her hands buried in her pants pockets, told Eliza she was wrong, that she needed to make breaks (otherwise no one could read it), but Eliza continued to connect the letters. There was no use in a secret swirling code if just anyone could read it and understand.

Her five-year old sister's training wheels seemed funny to her, the little bike, Eliza's own bike from two years ago, wobbling from left to right. Her light-skinned sister Toni didn't want to ride. Toni sat on her shins picking clover blossoms and putting them in a paper bag. On the too-small bike Eliza felt like a hand holding a pencil, leaning at an angle to the ground, off balance but held up by the tiny wheels. She had been riding without training wheels for such a long time, had gotten a new bike with a banana seat that was blue and said HUFFY, so riding this little one with her knees doubled up and those wheels on the back was funny. Twice, her weight caused her to topple over. This made Toni giggle.

"I'm fooling around, fool," Eliza said to her sister, brushing dirt and grass from her right knee, which had gone down hardest.

"You can't ride a bi-ike!" Toni sang, throwing clover with her chubby hands.

"Yeah, and you suck your thumb, I'm telling Daddy."

"Do not."

Toni sat on her thumb, which was swollen from her forgetful sucking. Eliza liked to tease Toni but would never tell on her to their parents. She picked up the bike and looked at their father kneeling by the side of the house. As her mother would say, he was *stressed out*. She would ask Mommy to tell him to relax because they loved each other. Even Toni who was only five understood about love. Eliza thought about riding over the grass, yelling, "Daddy, daddy, daddy, look!" She decided instead she'd take a turn off the driveway onto the smoother asphalt and see how far she could lean. Maybe the road would hold her leaning all the way, writing in cursive like a grown-up, *Tonitonitonieatstoads*.

In this family, Jeb was thinking, water spraying through three new pin-sized holes, you couldn't even trust anyone to put the girls to bed. He had come home late from Jiffy Lube the night before and found them all bunched together on the couch, Shante's arms around both kids, watching a rerun of *Three's Company*. It was ten o'clock. Jeb didn't know much about girls but a rule that stuck from his childhood was that children under eight ought to be in bed by eight. He hoped Shante was watching him struggle with the hose from the window. Teach her a lesson about responsibility.

Shante was, secretly, watching her husband from the kitchen window. In her hands she had two iron-ons for her girls, a butterfly and a sparkly star. She waited for the iron to heat up and spied on Jeb. It was thoughtful of him to water her garden although right now he did not look well. How tired he'd been the past year. But she had a nice thing as a surprise. She'd been talking to Eliza's teacher at Easton Elementary. They needed a Teacher's Aide. This was a job she could do. It didn't pay much, but it would help. Tonight she planned to tell Jeb. He would not have to work the overtime clean-up shift every night. They could go back to normal life, enjoy each other, be how they'd been before Jeb had gotten so eaten up by work. The iron was ready. She gazed at him outside the window, bent on one knee. When the Ford F-150 came barreling down the road she was thinking how much she loved her husband's shoulders, the straight, strong line of them against the lawn.

Gabriel Brooks had been in love with Rebecca since eighth grade and he knew that Senior Bash might be his last chance. He could tell her how much he wished she weren't going to college so far away. From the 7-11 they would head back to the party and if he could just get Nancy to walk ahead by herself toward the river, leaving him to steady Rebecca, hold her hand, then maybe something could happen. She was sitting in the front seat next to him, Nancy in the back. "You're so quiet," he said. "Something's up."

Rebecca took his arm. "I'm fine, you dope. I just want another beer." But when they got to Mindy's house, she said instead, "Shit, I just remembered, I got to go shopping with my dad."

"Right now?" (Gabriel was a little mad. Dr. Sperry, always ruining things. Like the time Gabe and Rebecca had rented *Say Anything*, and Dr. Sperry watched the entire movie with them.)

Rebecca put one of her dirty Birkenstocks on Gabe's dash. "Tomorrow morning, some graduation present."

"Come on, stay a while longer," Gabe said. "Look, Jenna and them just got here."

"Probably shoes, he says I need white shoes." She squeezed his arm, leaned back and kissed Nancy's cheek. "Drop me off at my truck."

"You okay?" they said to her in unison.

"Later, guys." She staggered out of the car.

On Saturday at eight-thirty in the morning, sipping coffee, Dr. Sperry was imagining the look on his daughter's face when they pulled up at Lednum's Jewelers. The ring he'd ordered for her was waiting there with pretty Janet Swann, the saleswoman who had recently married young Officer Bob Swann. The ring was a water-blue topaz set in gold with eight small diamonds. His daughter was going to love it.

"Dad?"

"In here watching the news. Ready to go?"

His daughter stumbled down the hall. "I had an accident yesterday."

Dr. Sperry checked his watch. Nine a.m., he'd told Janet Swann at Lednum's. "What kind of accident?"

"The truck, I think it's messed up."

He wouldn't think of the bottle caps Rebecca emptied from her pockets in her room, she collected those, she put them in a vase on her desk next to her silver-plated duck bank. Nancy Friend would never again want to think about Camels, or chilidogs, or Indian men. Gabriel Brooks, Nancy Friend, Marvin Ewing, Ina Fellows, the priest, the principal, the cops, the DA, the judge, and Dr. Sperry, and Rebecca herself, especially Rebecca, would not think about why she had chosen to drive away rather than check on the girl she'd hit. Why she'd hidden in her bedroom until next morning when she confessed to her father what she'd done. (Hadn't she and her father gone to the police themselves? Hadn't she complied with their requests? Wouldn't she suffer enough, this thing weighing on her for the rest of her life?)

"I think I hit something coming back from my friend's house."

"What friend? What, a tree?"

His daughter did not reply. She just stood there twisting a cord that came out of her shirt, a hood cord on her white and pink shirt, her face pale, almost bluish, the delicate skin around her eyes weepy.

"A dog? What? What did you hit?"

"I think I hit a girl. A little bicycle, like a tricycle, really small, oh Dad—"

With that, John Sperry's daughter sank into the floor.

Reversing her truck, not looking at the heap on the road, Rebecca had had a brief sense of a man stuck like a statue and a second, smaller child frozen on the lawn. A red bike bent into a body, a horrifying motionlessness like a question mark at the end of something. She had had a better, fuller understanding of her own legs shaking. Pulling onto the left side of the road, around the tangle lying there, she put her foot down hard on the gas pedal. Her father would be at the Pub. She flicked on headlights and slowed down. Why had the little kid swerved at the truck like that? She would be okay. How old was she, not dead, six? Nine? She couldn't be dead.

"Maybe it was a small deer," Dr. Sperry said slowly. He knelt over his daughter, checking her forehead for fever. "A deer could have leaped into your path. But is it possible you hit a girl? I'm sure everything will be okay."

Rebecca, driving wildly on the darkened country roads, would always remember how she felt a sort of looseness in her jaw. As if her jaw were hanging unattached, like spit, the rest of her head compact and controlled but this jaw disobedient, foreign. She couldn't take her hands off the wheel to wipe her mouth because she needed them to guide the truck, racing toward home. Once she was safe in her room with her duck bank and her lacrosse stick, her desk covered with forms from the college where she was heading in the fall, her vanity and the music box that had belonged to her dead mother, she would look in the mirror and check her jaw.

On her forehead she felt her father's cool fingers. Pushing into her right ear and cheekbone and shoulder was the plush rug. One elbow stuck out at a graceless angle. Her trunk and legs, crooked, felt as numb as if they belonged to someone else. Rebecca kept her eyes shut tight and thought of all the brightness ahead of her.

Eliza's last thoughts before the truck hit involved the complicated process of light fading on the road. The road was a tablet for her cursive self, growing less and less distinct in the dusk. Her father called for her, she'd be sure to kiss Daddy ten times before she went to bed, calling her name, "Elizaelizaelizaeliza," why such a pull in his voice? Then the chrome grate was coming, and the glass windshield, and the loudest roar. The white girl's face behind the windshield, above a cherry-colored hood, over the gravel asphalt pad, all wide-eyed and blank. Eliza's last idea might have told her that the surrounding soybeans and field corn of Talbot County and Dorchester County and all the counties stretching away for as far as she would ever see had turned with the slant of her body, writing; that this big girl's ghost face had already flown into her and away from her; that everything in the world connected under her into cursive for *milesmilesmilesmilesmiles.*

HALF LIFE

EVERY MORNING, Amber ate cornflakes at the white plastic table on a white plastic chair with her hard, single-issue, white plastic spoon. She ate cornflakes and drank weak coffee and thought about her two bras with underwire removed from the cups, and her eight pairs of underpants, and the six chain-link fences that subdivided C-Pod, and the window in her cell with four horizontal bars. She used to contemplate her cellmate, Fran, hunched over toast on the far side of C-Pod, but ever since the shower incident, she just kept her eyes on her bowl and considered how she had never, ever, given cornflakes to her daughter. She and Crissy were strictly donut girls, she thought, which took her mind off C-Pod. She needed to focus on what *had been*, before this all began: reading books to Crissy on the shag rug, brewing her own coffee every morning, spooning sugar from the pretty bowl painted with music notes. She'd only be in the TCCF for twenty-one months, while Fran had life.

Amber's first morning, the smell of disinfectant hanging in the air, she'd asked Fran, "What'd you do to end up here?" That was five weeks ago, before she knew anything. They still lay in bed after the CO's call. The ceiling of their cell was beige. Fran, tall, large-headed and paunchy, was fifty-five or maybe sixty, with bad skin and a frizz of gray hair. Their space in the Talbot County Correctional Facility was the size of a large bathroom with one vent, one porcelain sink, one open toilet, two bunks, two shelves, and a barred window looking out on a defunct sewing factory. At Amber's question, Fran had gotten up without a word. She stood to change her underwear, and Amber tried not to stare. Fran had pancake boobs. Her abdomen flapped like an empty water balloon.

When Fran didn't answer, Amber asked, "Cat got your tongue?" with a small smile, as she might have teased her daughter.

Fran's hunch called attention to her height. "Nothing," she rasped. "Don't you fucking know?"

Five words. Later that morning, in the exercise room, Amber had heard the scoop on Fran. Killed her husband—and not in self-defense—she'd gone nuts, a woman named Elsa told Amber by the free weights. Fran had done time at Jessup, the maximum-security state prison, and she'd gotten transferred back to Talbot County for her appeal, trying to get second-degree lowered to criminally negligent homicide. If the appeal failed, she'd head back to Jessup to wait it out, twenty-five to life. The female inmates were let into the exercise room in groups of five. Elsa talked, and the other three women nodded and agreed, Fran was bad news.

But that first morning, as Amber tucked hospital corners, following Fran's lead, she'd persisted, "How *long* you been here?"

It was so early, six AM, with darkness leaking through the bars on their window and fluorescent bulbs whitening the cell while the Correction Officer rounded. In other cells, inmates turned under their blankets, slapped water on their faces, coughed and spit, urinated in stained cell toilets. Fran stood at the door, waiting for the CO to do the headcount.

"I'm only wondering," Amber said.

Fran cracked her neck. "Six months I been here."

"Here? Where were you before?"

"I killed a girl like you, just shut the fuck up."

On the outside, alarm clocks rang, coffee dripped, and school buses roared to life in Talbot County's still-dark soybean fields. Amber imagined that somewhere in Easton, a morning streetlamp died. Flickered, then canceled its circle of light.

Talbot County Correctional Facility, just six years old, had lights and video cameras at every angle. There were three televisions that blared soap operas in the main section, one in the exercise room. The shining chain-link fence created four smaller areas. Glass observation rooms lined the clean concrete walls. There was always the smell of new paint. That first day, Amber had been taught the rigid schedule of making bunks and straightening cells. Breakfast in C-Pod's main communal area, clean-up, free time, outdoor rec, lunch, clean-up, afternoon lockdown for the CO shift change, supper, clean-up. Amber's first supper was canned carrots and overdone chicken, which she ate with her only piece of tableware, the hard-plastic spoon. After clean-up came free time before bed. Beside Amber's narrow bunk, under the fresh cover of off-white, she read the etchings of previous inmates. A calendar, all the days X'd out. *Screw Rick. You Lam Ass. Fran is a Bitch.* Amber got out her two photographs of Crissy from under her bed. One from seven years ago, the day they'd come home from the hospital, Crissy's sweet face all red and shiny. The other from Easton Elementary, her daughter upside-down on a swing, hair sweeping the dirt. Both pictures were in an envelope on which Crissy had printed in pencil, *FOR MOM.*

Just before lockdown, Fran came into the cell, kicked the flusher on the toilet, and lay down, piling the blanket on her head. Amber stared at her and then put away her pictures. She counted up. Fran said twenty-one words that first day. She would utter a total of forty-six over the next five weeks, up until the spoon.

The longer Amber was inside, the more she focused on numbers. The spoon came as an ugly surprise.

AMBER FINISHED her cornflakes and added more sugar to her coffee. Her own punishment of twenty-one months was actually two consecutive sentences, one for a year, and another for nine months. It was taking a while to figure the full meaning of all that time. Next month was April, and she would turn twenty-five, and it would be two birthdays from now before she was out. Crissy would be nine. Amber had taught her daughter how to add and subtract—a dozen donuts, what happens when you take out two? With five weeks subtracted, thirty-five days, seventy-nine weeks of her sentence remained.

The public defender said it could have been worse. The judge could have found Amber guilty of a felony, rather than a serious misdemeanor, and could have ruled three to six years' incarceration at a state prison. Worse? Amber closed her eyes. Her daughter had been placed in a foster home to live with strangers. They'd lost the apartment and all their belongings. All the rich people in

Talbot County seemed to be members of the same country club, and the same two churches, so no one would trust Amber to clean houses after this.

Two weeks ago, Channel 17 News had done a story on Easton Elementary School. As Amber held her breath, the camera panned over children, white and black, jumping rope and playing rock-paper-scissors. Crissy hadn't appeared on the news, and the foster parents hadn't brought her for a visit. How tall had her daughter grown? Was she doing okay in school? Amber doubted that the public defender had a clue about worse.

The fifty women in the jail shared close quarters. C-Pod had been designed to house only twenty-six prisoners, but Talbot County had a variance to double-cell the women while another unit was being built. Pretty quickly, Amber recognized all the women in forest green uniforms. She thought of them in terms of the number of months in their sentences. Patti and Robin, next cell over, were 8 and 10. Elsa, in for possession, her third time in jail, had 21 months, like Amber. A couple meth-heads wore orange uniforms that meant they hadn't yet been sentenced. Only Fran was in for so many years.

When Amber asked a CO how many inmates lived in Maryland, he told her it was around twenty-five thousand. Almost half a percent of Marylanders behind bars. He mentioned the Women's Correctional in Jessup. Someone else—2, a pregnant woman—said there were six hundred prisoners at Jessup. "What are you here for, anyway?" 2 asked Amber.

"Bad luck," Amber said, shortly. Because 2 would be gone so soon, Amber didn't bother to go into details.

She'd gone back to her cell. She spent a lot of time in the cell, silently, with Fran, growing used to the older woman's tics. Morning and night, Fran splashed water on her face and underarms and then swiped it onto the floor. Four splashes, four swipes. In bed, she scratched herself in threes. One, two, three scratches on the right shoulder blade, and one, two, three on the neck. The snoring that followed made concentric ripples of sound, which lulled Amber to sleep.

There had been one night it was eight splashes, eight swipes, and water all over the floor. One, two, three, four, five scratches on the upper arms, and one, two, three, four on the thighs. Before the snoring began, Fran had shifted and hissed in the dark, "I didn't kill any girl."

Amber rolled over. "What?"

"I raped my shitty husband," Fran croaked. "What a life."

Thirteen words, just after lights-out.

AMBER SWALLOWED her lukewarm coffee and glanced across the common area. Fran was buttering toast with the back of her spoon. Amber looked away. When she got out of jail, she and Crissy would move down to Florida. Amber rehearsed this plan so often in her head, she believed it was true. But before that, there were seven hours in the cell per day, and weeks of seven days. Seventy-nine weeks. Seven times seven times seventy-nine, a thing expanding upward and outward. Above it all towered twenty-one months of concrete, steel, and brick. The limit of twenty-one turned out to be not where it touched sky but where the concrete began.

Across the room, Fran scratched her gray head. Amber suspected that Fran had lice. Every day, Amber checked herself over in the shower. The water sprayed hot and hard, much better than the pressure in her own bathroom, the shower she'd never see again. Three mornings ago, her thirty-second morning in jail, she had been second in line for the shower, first after Fran. She imagined Fran, inside the white box, swiping her flabby arms. Seven swipes, eight swipes, nine. Amber had thought of butterflies, and her daughter's blueberry-colored comb. Ten. Eleven. Twelve. She missed Crissy so much. Were the foster parents good to her? Thirteen, fourteen, fifteen. Suddenly, Amber felt herself dizzy, slipping. She lurched forward into the opening shower door and heard someone bark, "Watch it!"

To head off a confrontation, someone in Control darkened the main lights in C-Pod.

A strong grip, flesh on flesh. Hands caught her from falling, but in the dim green emergency light, Amber couldn't see anything. It didn't take the COs long to relight the overheads, only seconds, but whoever had supported Amber let go. In front of her, Amber saw only the empty white box. Ten minutes later, 3, a sentenced meth kid, told Amber it had been Fran, wrapped in towels, who jumped out to catch her.

So that afternoon in the exercise yard, Amber had walked toward Fran, who hunched by the perimeter fence, looking toward the old sewing factory. Some women—10, 11, and 18—played basketball.

Amber coughed once. "I know you helped me," she said. "Thanks."

A basketball rolled toward them on the ground. Fran bit a hangnail on her thumb, her pocked skin looking worse in the full sun.

"When I get out of here," Amber said, "I'm gonna take my daughter and move south to Florida where I was born." Overhead, barbed wire coiled. Two seagulls perched. 10 retrieved the ball, threw it back into play. The bell rang, and the officers called them in. Fran walked toward the courtyard door. She stopped suddenly. Amber bumped right into her back, and the old woman whipped around.

"My husband wouldn't leave me alone, so I killed him," she yelled. Then she called over to the two officers. "Little bitch is threatening me," she said, motioning at Amber. "Carrying filed steel off the coffee vat."

Amber's skin went rubbery as the female CO patted her down, and Fran disappeared along the hall. "Don't give us any trouble," the officer warned. "Next time it'll be a strip search." Amber had counted squares on the floor and come to her new, firm resolve: Don't *ever* talk to Fran.

THE COMMON AREA was the color of cornflakes. Amber drank the last of her milk from the bowl. One, two, three women got up from their tables, cleared their places, and wiped down chairs. It would be easy to move down South. Maybe they wouldn't go to Florida, maybe they'd stop in some other state, North Carolina or Georgia, a city with richer people and fancier houses. Amber would be smarter and work harder when she got out of here. She would tell Crissy about the horizontal window, the right-angle corridors, the concrete walls. How jail tightened you in. How numbers could be friendly, or they could hit with sharp edges. How one o'clock stabbed your foot. Five rammed your stomach. Eleven bashed your head with bars. She'd make sure Crissy didn't end up like her. She'd tell Crissy how stretching arms or legs was like performing an act of flesh against math.

As the morning television droned, Amber was gripped by a sudden rage. How dare Fran lie to get her in trouble? They'd shared so few words. Across the tables of the common area now, she met her cellmate's eyes, dark and sunken. As Amber thought about what she could do to retaliate against Fran, one of Fran's eyes winked at her. Holding her plastic spoon in her right hand, like a white flag, Fran waved.

Then she gripped the spoon and drew it forcefully down across her bare bicep, and an angry red mark appeared, a line of blood.

Fran walked to the breakfast cart, then toward their cell, left hand holding the spoon. Her right hand cupped her upper arm. Amber took her own tray to the cart. She counted fifteen dirty mugs including her own. She counted four coffee stains on a dishtowel. She counted eight cornflakes spilled on the floor. When she went to the cell, Fran was not there. Her towel was gone. On the floor was a tiny blood smear. Amber rummaged through Fran's belongings. Two bras. Three soup packets. Five pairs of socks. No sharpened plastic spoon.

From under her own bed, Amber pulled out her photographs and looked for details she might have missed: the reflection in her newborn's eyes, the swing at school, hair in the dirt, the envelope marked *FOR MOM*. When the hour came for outdoor recreation, Fran still hadn't returned to the cell. Amber got in line. Outside the shower area, flip-flops on her feet, hair dripping, stood Fran.

"I'm not going out," Fran announced. "I need to lie down."

The CO led Fran back to the cell.

Out on the yard with the other women, Amber kept quiet about the spoon. Above, stainless steel looped against the sky. The sky, through the helical coils of razor wire, filled the number eight over and over again, crisp blue through spiraling steel. Her daughter would be eight soon. In twenty-one months, a quarter of Crissy's life would pass. Amber craned her neck to see seagulls and her neck constricted, the eight like a noose pulling up. The midday dinner was chicken that Amber ate with her hands. Fran did not come out of the cell. Amber sat in the common area. She would have liked to use the payphone but there was no one to call. After supper, she told 21, Elsa, about Fran's arm. Elsa whistled, a low siren that caused the CO to stare in their direction. "Girl," Elsa said, "she's filed it down on the walls. Stay away from that crazy bitch."

When the bells rang for lockdown, Amber returned to the cell. Fran sat cross-legged in bed. Amber sank under her covers and stared at the beige ceiling. Outside the cell door, C-Pod readied for headcount. Women shuffled by. The overhead lights bore down.

"What's wrong with you?" Fran said.

Amber's neck snapped. Fran's face looked relaxed, as if the interior muscles had sprung loose. She spoke again, her voice like a hinge. "Don't answer. Let me tell you something. *Nothing* was my husband's fault."

Amber stared. "Why'd you kill him, then?"

"Didn't kill him, he killed me," Fran said. Her eyes were puffy. "Why are you here?"

"Fraud," Amber said. She had been waiting to say this for a long time. "I took checkbooks from people I cleaned for. I forged signatures. Eighteen thousand dollars."

The CO knocked for headcount. Amber leapt out of bed, and Fran stood beside her. The CO on the other side of the glass window nodded at them. Fran's shoulders shuddered. The shudder caught her under the arms. She was laughing.

"I can see you," Fran said. Her lips curled like a dog's. "Little house cleaner for rich folk. What'd you make, about nine thousand a year? Those bruises your daddy gave your mother still sitting under your skin, and in your baby's eyes. You get pregnant in high school? Shows in the photos. I bet he said he loved fake blondes, and blue mascara, and new heels from K-mart. Yeah, and then the boy disappears, you have your baby and sit around watching television at Momma's place, then figure out you have to *do something.*"

Amber, open-mouthed, sucked in like she'd been punched.

Fran leaned over fiercely. "Proud of your baby girl?"

Headcount complete, the overheads blinked off. Amber waited to adjust to the light of the moon coming in the quadruple-barred window. The emergency bulbs shone faintly green. She counted seconds.

Fran's voice filled the cell. "My man," she said. "His name was Ron. He played softball at the park, had plenty of friends before he got laid off. But when he was at home, even when he still had his job, he'd just lay there, doing nothing. Can you imagine? *Nothing.* The only time we ever touched was me hitting him for doing nothing. Which I got sick of. It started small, I'd pinch his arm, make him get off his ass, but I got sicker and sicker of it. When he quit work, the only time he got off our fat white couch was if one of his buddies called. Otherwise he'd sit there on the couch like he was made of it. Once when I was yelling, he put a pillow over his head so he didn't have to hear. I grabbed what was next to me, it was a lamp. I swung it and broke his ankle. He was on crutches after that, so you see how he did *nothing* to me. But I got so mad I couldn't breathe. One night, him sitting there on the couch, bent, like he was holding his head on with his hands, I grabbed his softball bat next to the door. I just meant to scare him, you know, shake him out of his misery. But he didn't wake up, and the police came before I could call them. Nothing ever hurt me like him just sitting there. They said murder. I retched and retched. I thought they were meaning Ron killed me."

When Fran stopped talking, there was zero sound in the cell. Amber held the concrete walls and felt them sweating. She stumbled over to her bed. That idiot DA was so wrong. It was worse. It had been worse since Amber was four, and she and her mother ran away from Florida and her father. It had been worse from New York City to Philadelphia to Dover, where it was worse, her mother working nights at a club she wouldn't let Amber see, and Fran was right, it was worse when Amber got pregnant, and it was worse yet when her mother passed away.

"Since then," Fran said, "it's so fucking old. They'll move me back to Jessup and by the time my case comes up again, I'll have been in half my life."

Amber thought of Fran's hands catching her. She remembered herself pregnant, big as a house, her mother with cancer. Losing her fulltime at the K-mart. Moving to Easton with her baby. Getting work cleaning large, vacant estates on the river, and stealing all that money to pay rent and buy a blue shag rug, a butterfly shower curtain, a sugar bowl made of glass.

"I been practicing with the spoon," Fran said. "Cutting, you know. It's sharp. It's under your bed where you keep your pictures.

I could cut a jugular with that thing and then hide it in my cunt."

Amber lay on her bunk over a sharpened spoon next to a woman who'd killed her husband for doing nothing. Amber waited and waited, but Fran didn't say more.

AMBER ENVISIONED TIME like a streetlamp blinking off that night. Imagine the darkness. Imagine Fran creeping out of her bunk to retrieve her strange weapon. Imagine her kneeling by the cell door. Imagine Fran knocking when the officer rounds. The officer opening the door. Both her arms swooping in a move that is ungainly like an old cat. The edge slips into the officer's neck, the softness between his ear and esophagus. He crumples, Fran steals his keys and dashes to the door, and the video cameras do not pick her up in the dark. The door is open. The CO is on the floor. He moans.

Amber lay and waited. Soon, Fran snored in the moonlight. The blanket over her chest rose and fell. Amber thought about seventeen years already in jail. She thought about twenty-five more. She thought about life. She counted the snores. In the morning after the CO unlocked the cells, 11 reported blood on a white plastic chair. Questioning followed an immediate lockdown. 21 said, "Check Fran." They searched the cell and found, in Amber's personal box, the sharpened spoon. "What's going on, what's this?" they said.

Fran's eyes, dark zeroes, blazed. "Assholes," she said. She rolled up her sleeves. "You think you know it all, here's a surprise. Here's what you like to miss."

Fresh scrapes bled on Fran's flabby arms. Before the COs could react, Fran jerked down her pants, and the red lines on her thighs reached north and south, long horrible trails. One of the officers grabbed Fran. Amber gasped as the other guard moved toward her.

"Amber didn't have nothing to do with it," Fran said.

They took Fran to the upper deck: twenty-eight days of keep-lock. No commissary, no television, no blanket or sheet during daytime. No showers but for once a week while the others were outside on the yard. No contact with anyone. A week into the se-questering, Amber asked the older CO, Mike, about Fran. He said she wasn't eating. She just lay in bed. Amber asked if Mike would take Fran a message, but that was against the rules. "Is she going back to Jessup?" Amber asked.

"Yeah, I guess she will," Mike said. "Her appeal fell through."

FRAN RETURNED TO THE CELL in May. It was the nighttime glare just before lights-out. In the yard the number eight noosed. Be-yond, the bulbs in streetlamps expired, and were replaced, ex-pired, and were replaced. Amber was in bed, looking at Crissy up-side-down on the swing. Fran's bad skin gleamed. Her eyes opened and closed like the cell. Out in C-Pod, the officer rounded. Amber rose and stood by Fran, and then she helped Fran to her bunk. Fran said nothing when Amber caressed the spoon-cut scars. Four doz-en women breathed beneath blankets. One vomited in the toilet. Another coughed three times before lights-out. Amber pulled up Fran's blanket and stretched it over the old woman's finite frame.

THE JANET SWANN SHOW

DO YOU REMEMBER how that morning long ago in the future the Holiday Inn lobby chirped with early risers, and on the other side of the wall of glass you could see the parking lot in Missoula, Montana? Do you remember? Can you see it now? How the background music swelled, your shaggy blond husband Bob worked out in the fitness room, and you, Janet Swann, dipped your toes in the water. An indoor pool of questions. For example: why at twenty-nine did your thighs pancake as you sat on that concrete lip? What were you looking for, gazing into that ocean of cars? You and Bob had flown there for your aunt's funeral, and then the next morning you stared out the windows at a stranger's creamy skin, a red scarf, her green-and-blue patterned purse with something squirming inside.

It was not television, it was real life, Janet Swann, and what you didn't know was vast!

YOU KNEW how an old TV worked. You'd seen it on *Law and Order* as you lay next to Bob, the night before, in your king-sized bed. When an image is broken into an assortment of small dots, the human brain reintegrates. Bob said he took apart a cathode ray tube once. He started going into detail, but you told him you'd like to watch the show, no offense.

Why did you insist on attending the funeral of an aunt you barely knew?

THAT MORNING when the stranger unzipped her purse, out popped a funny dog. Do you remember how you almost laughed, and thought, *David Letterman,* the pug who moaned *I love you?* It licked the arms of the woman who looked like an extra from *Dollhouse* and also like a prettier version of a foster cousin you'd met for the first time at your aunt's funeral. Your Aunt Mary had raised foster children, had you known that before? The dog's eyes rolled as the pretty stranger dropped it in the trunk of her Mercedes. The indoor pool was square like your diamond ring, the blue of a brochure selling honeymoons to Cancun.

Should you and Bob have bought a dog? Would that have fixed anything?

SOMEWHERE in the lobby a guest laughed like a rooster, and outside the window the red scarf fluttered on the young woman's neck, and the poor dog tried to leap from her trunk. Beyond, the lot stretched to highway and Montana's mountains, crouching stark as dawn. You compared them to the flatness of your hometown. In the fitness room adjacent to you, Bob pedaled his stationary bike, two years younger than you and so diligent about working out. You meant to swim a few laps, but you sat instead, dry in your ivory suit. Your hands were numb. Your toes dipped into the blue pool. Bob waved, and you waved back, feeling a sense of disassociation, it being the most time you had spent with Bob since your honeymoon.

Did you think you and he would have children?

OUTSIDE THE WINDOW on the other side of a hedge from the pretty woman, a black man, tall and trim, removed his blazer. He wore button cuffs and front-creased slacks. He untied his tie. He balled it up. Bob's head poked around the corner. "Honey, how you doing?" he asked. You gave him thumbs-up. When the night before Bob had asked what you remembered about your father's elder sister, you never really answered. "I'm watching the show, Bob," you'd told him.

Someone in the lobby with a voice like a grackle said, *Checking out?*

AUNT MARY had come back to the Eastern Shore once, for your father's funeral, when you were fifteen. You were drawn to her red hair and purple dress. *Always an outsider,* your mother said. When you were little, you wanted to touch your aunt's paintings, the one like a blue city, another like enormous blades of grass. You secretly ran your fingers around the surface of a green curve and found it felt like skin. At the funeral, a stranger played hammer dulcimer on the lawn. A woman named Olive shared Mary's house, a log two-story with views of a stream. You wept so hard over the ashes that you felt embarrassed, but you couldn't seem to stop. Aunt Mary had painted your father as a boy, riding a red bicycle, his hand and face two thin blurs.

Janet Swann, back when you were nearly thirty, how many years do you have left to live?

A DRAWER in a lobby desk squawked. You were still sitting on the edge, your legs now in the pool. In the parking lot, the trunked pug licked the woman's hand. She might have been crying. On the other side of the hedge, the man removed his cuffed shirt, and underneath, his dark skin was no color you could name. He slipped off his dress shoes and his socks. What is happening out there? Up close, small phosphorus dots of excited green, red, and blue do not make sense. According to *Law and Order*, old-fashioned televisions work because, at a distance, the brain forces dots into pictures. Across the lot from you, an old woman emerged from a blue station wagon. She looked like your high school English teacher, that one who was bonkers for Walt Whitman, what was her name? Out of the blue station wagon, the woman's hair flew in every direction. She pulled books and papers from the back and stacked them on the ground. She shook her head, muttering to herself. You forgot about the pug, the undressing man, the funeral, and Bob, and you watched the piles of novels and notebooks and newspapers growing over the ground. People with roller suitcases stared, too. Just the day before, you'd cried over Aunt Mary's ashes and again in front of her paintings. Horses in an enclosure on the lawn's edge had whinnied as you watched the sky and cried. The sky was the phosphorescent blue of the ribbon your aunt tied in your hair when she stayed after your father died.

You were barely aware of Bob. What you didn't know was like a pool.

BOB SPOKE to someone in the fitness room. A small girl, her mother watching from a plastic chair, jumped off the concrete edge. Your legs, refracted in the moving water, didn't belong to you. If you divide a moving scene into a series of pictures and show them in quick succession, your brain will construct a single scene, like solving a crime. "That's interesting," Bob had concluded after *Law and Order.* He'd taken his vitamins, you'd removed your contacts, and you both put pillows over your head as he murmured, "I love you."

What you didn't know was how to get perspective.

OUTSIDE, shirtless and barefoot, the business man unbuckled his belt, while the young woman across the hedge held the trunk at one inch of breathing space for the pug, and the old woman dumped paperbacks on the ground. The young woman lost her grasp on the trunk, the pug jumped, and the business man's pants fell to the ground. The pug dashed toward the old woman. *Rip, riff, rit,* it barked. Dropping playbills and poetry, the old woman swooped up the dog. You were riveted.

Where was all of it getting you?

THE YOUNG WOMAN ran after her dog as the old woman furrowed her brow. Heading toward the highway across the lot, the nearly naked man heard the barking, and he turned, as if electrified. He scissored the space with his long legs, covered a third of the distance, then half, then three-fourths, and he puts out his arms, and the young woman lunges. You feel a hand grasp your shoulder! "Honey," Bob says. But you can't take your eyes off the window, off the young woman leaning, grasping the man's naked hands! Does she know him? Are they in love? Is the dog *their* dog? Bob's saying, "Maybe I'll call in—" and when the old woman gets in her car, but it's not her dog, you think, and you're so confused, "—so if you'd like to stay—" and the grackle in the lobby squawks, *Can I help you?*

Oh, Janet Swann, back then! His lips are right there, close to yours, his face aglow, what did he just say? In the parking lot, the others move off scene. *Through me many long dumb voices*, you remember from somewhere. The show is about to end. Bob's eyes are still warm. Would TV characters kiss? I tell you now, if you understand anything about the past or present or future, pull your lover close and jump yourselves into that pool.

Dead Man

THE YEAR MY FATHER walked off, I thought often about the spring I was eight when we lived on the creek below Suicide Bridge Road, and my mother had died, and I found a dead man in my woods.

I can still see the ravine where the monkey vines grew as thick as mooring; where you could climb the double-trunked elm over to the level branches of a beech; where under a netting of honeysuckle and greenbrier lay rotting tires, belts, bale feeders, pallets, and the hull of a milk-truck; where beneath the root system of a wind-toppled white oak, surrounded by low mayapples, I built my fort. I cleared the ground of debris, laid a blanket of dry leaves, and decorated with treasures I found in the woods. A mason jar, a small icebox missing its door, a strip of chrome, an Indian pottery shard. I found the dead man, an old man, older than my father, lying on his back in my fort. Dead, I say now, because we never spoke, the man and I, and he never moved, which is proof enough of death. But that spring, and for a long time after, I figured he was alive because he, a solid ghost, or a wood sprite, or maybe just a hallucination, looked as if he were asleep.

The ravine led to the creek that led to the Choptank River, which separated Talbot from Dorchester County. After snowmelt and rains, the ravine would carry field runoff down to the creek. I used to wade through the streams, kicking through branches and collecting stones. At the base of the ravine, an orange-clay mouth spouted water from underground. It was ice cold. If you stood barefoot, the freezing ran up your legs to your back into your head, where it balled into an ache, and you would step out quickly and shake like a dog.

It was late April when I found him. His knees were covered with dried mud. I remember thinking how he must've crawled there from who knows how far away. When he woke he'd be hungry, so I piled ripe mayapples next to his mouth. My mother, Virginia Gowe Taylor, had been raised in Dorchester County and had taught me about her native plants. Mayapples, also called Indian apple and Devil's apple, have lemon-yellow berries, the only part of the plant that is edible. I arranged some jack-in-the-pulpits in a rusted tin can. Their bulbous spokes and green-and-purple stripes are poisonous through and through, so I didn't leave those near the man's head. I left them by his feet, on a flat stone. Atop, a little note: "*Don't eat. Your friend, Lucinda.*"

"I suppose dinner, as a concept, is not far away?" my father asked, smoking his pipe and sighing out smoke. "It's your job now, Lucy. I need your help around here."

My father was a man with a gray, somber face, large in his dark suits. Every day he drove an hour and a half up to Preston, over through Easton, then across the Bay Bridge to Annapolis to run the business *his* father had owned, the Ernest R. Taylor Funeral Home. It was right off Church Circle, around the corner from the State House. Ever since my mother's funeral, my father had wanted me to act more like an adult. Quickly, I learned to make pancakes, bake potatoes, test spaghetti for doneness. My father was quite serious. Serious and sad. I can't remember if this started before my mother died, or after.

During dinner chores, my father related the day's news. He had been involved that week in a disappearance, an elderly friend of his, a renowned architect named Walter Grinestaff, who had suddenly gone missing. Walter's daughter Fiona, a B-movie actress out in California, had been telephoning since Sunday. At dinner, my father read aloud yet another newspaper article about his friend. My father read slowly, rubbing his eyes.

"The search for a body continues with aid from Coast Guard and oyster trawlers," he intoned. "First time the Blue Angels ever flew over the bridge walk, Lucy. How you like them apples?"

I was frightened of my father, more than I let on, so during dinner I usually didn't talk at all. He didn't like me playing in the woods, warned me away from poison ivy, black widow spiders, copperhead snakes, and wild dogs; a pack of wild dogs had once been reported in Talbot County, according to his friends at the country club. So I told him nothing of the old man in my fort. While I ate the last of my Brussels sprouts, my father, smoking, took out his knife and scored the edges of the article about Mr. Grinestaff.

"One for the hopper, Lucy," he said, tucking it into his shirt pocket where he kept his tobacco pouch. The hopper was my father's box of saved things. He pulled two Hershey bars out of a drawer in the bureau. "I know it's no dessert for a lady," he said, "but here you go."

I didn't eat mine because there was someone in the woods who needed it.

EIGHTEEN YEARS LATER, and like a time-lapsed, mirrored image of Walter Grinestaff, my father left no note. He walked away and never came back. The police were notified, but other than checking in hospitals and morgues, there was not much they could do. I kept returning to the same bench on State Circle, four blocks from my father's house. I sorted through my father's papers and came across the Grinestaff clipping. The edges were tattered and browned, and it smelled of smoke. Every so often I pulled it out, as if it were a clue my father planted.

The Star-Republican, Tuesday, May 4, 1982

**Annual Crossing Raises Concerns
Prominent Architect Missing**

On Sunday, architect and philanthropist Walter G. Grinestaff set out to walk across the Chesapeake Bay Bridge that was part of his life's work. At the suspension tower, the highest section of the 4.3-mile eastbound span, he suffered an apparent heart attack. Bridge Walk Volunteers radioed for help, but before the arrival of Kent Island Emergency Services, Mr. Grinestaff disappeared. Police have found no trace of the seventy-year old man. Family members, daughter Fiona Grinestaff of California, and Henry Barth, son of the late Nennie Barth Grinestaff, wait for notice.

"We don't suspect foul play," said Kent Island Police Chief Dallas Gray.

Chairman of the yearly Bridge Walk, Paul Bowdle, confirms that all Sunday's participants have been questioned. The volunteer who radioed 911, recognizing Mr. Grinestaff, shouted to others to carry water to the collapsed man but no one could locate the victim. Bystanders were directed to keep walking. No witnesses of Mr. Grinestaff's disappearance have been found.

Chief Gray suspects the elderly architect may have stumbled over the bridge's 354-foot high railing. From her Hollywood home, Fiona Grinestaff expressed similar concerns. The search for a body continues with aid from Coast Guard and oyster trawlers. The accident has given shape to fears about the safety of the annual walk. Bridge Walk organizers assert that precautions will be in place by next year. "Accidents can be prevented," Bowdle stated. This was the first year the Blue Angels performed during the Bridge Walk. Fred Callaway, representing Governor Hughes, stressed in a statement to the press, "We're limiting access to railings, posting safety warnings, and planning further investigation into the matter."

I HAD AN ACTIVE IMAGINATION as a child. The night I found the man, it rained, and I imagined a giant flood in my ravine, the dead man floating higher and higher and being carried out to sea. Then, I imagined the rain making him sprout like an old potato putting down roots into the soil of my fort. Next morning, my father was off without a word, and before catching the yellow school bus, I ran down to the fort.

He lay in there, glistening like something that could either spring up with clenched fists or start to melt. Now when I close my eyes, I can still see the shine of waxy lips and loose jowls. On his left wrist, he wore a silver watch. On his right pinky, a diamond ring. The top of his head shone, bald but for a few white strings of hair. His face was softly wrinkled.

"Can I see your ring?" It glided easily off his pale, loose finger.

My father wore a diamond pinky ring, too, which had belonged to his father, Ernest R. Taylor, Senior. I told the old man I was putting a Hershey bar in the little icebox, if he wanted it.

FOR DINNER that night my father and I ate pork chops and potatoes. My father mentioned that we should finally move back to Annapolis, so I would stop playing in the woods and learn to be a lady. He didn't wait for me to answer. "In other news, the space shuttle is scheduled to make its first flight in September," he said. "Won't that be a thing to see."

I played with my food. "I don't want to leave here."

"Lucy, we're not going to argue at dinner. Put this out of your mind." He lit his pipe and ignored me for the rest of the night.

THE OLD MAN hadn't touched the mayapples nor the chocolate when I went back the next morning. His head, looking so delicate, reminded me of down I found in our bluebird house after chasing out a black snake. By the third morning, some animal, probably a raccoon, had taken the candy bar; I found the brown and silver wrapping down by the spring. I imagined the raccoons standing in moonlight, washing their food. After it rained again on the fourth night, my fort smelled of earthworms and tea. I told the old man he needed protection from the elements, and when the sun dried the rain, I dragged down a piece of plywood from my father's woodpile and with the broken icebox I propped up a roof to cover his body. In the honeysuckle and greenbrier growing up around my fort, he lay like a baby in a forest crib.

I MOVED BACK to Maryland that spring my father walked off to take a job at an Annapolis law firm. I worked from dawn until dusk, but when I called in one night to explain that my father had disappeared, the senior partners told me to take time off. For a week, I read through the hopper twice, three, four times. My father had treated it as a sort of reliquary, or legacy, and with that blank of time, what else was there to do? I found a letter from Walter Grinestaff's daughter, Fiona. Was it saved there for my eyes? When I read it, the dead man's lack of emotion, his cool passivity, his refusal to engage, came rushing back to me.

June 15, 1982

Ernest R. Taylor Funeral Home Inc.
144 Duke of Gloucester Street
Annapolis, Maryland 21401

Dear Ernie Junior:

I write again to request your professional assistance. As you know, Walter has not been found—I conclude he has stepped off this mortal coil to another plane of existence. What I should write is, *Barely can I contemplate the loss of my dear father, his influence on Annapolis, the state of Maryland, our capitol Washington, D.C., and all of America, an unforgettable man. We have lost a treasure in he who sleeps; and, by a sleep, I mean to say we end the heart-ache, the thousand natural shocks...*

However, dear Ernie, despite its status as a local mystery, my father's disappearance surprised none less than me. Walter was not well. One month after losing Nennie (beloved *fourth* wife), my father learned of his failing heart. I have no doubt that on May 2, Sunday of his and Nennie's anniversary, he swan-dived into the Chesapeake.

That his body has not been found is troubling, turning honorable pomp and circumstance into a can of worms. What if somehow my father survived? Can you presume the death of a missing bridge-jumper, and if so, how soon? September would make a proper Maryland memorial month. After October, I won't be able to make it home, due to the premier of my new film.

This brings me to the second worm in the can: Will we see the players well bestowed? As you most likely know, Walter wrote me out of the will. For choosing "the business" over his business, I didn't inherit a cent; all the money will go to Nennie's son Henry, mentally retarded and cared for by an opportunist. So who will pay for the great man's entombment? Do not worry yourself, Ernie; despite everything directing me to the contrary, I will spare no expense.

Third worm: there is no note nor record of Walter's intent to kill himself, but should one appear, would the E. R. Taylor home still accept this business and arrange a proper burial for an old friend?

Please do reply at your earliest convenience.

Cordially,

Fiona

MORNINGS BEFORE SCHOOL, a moist glow emanated from the man's uncovered forehead. It might have been dew lit by the sun penetrating through forest canopy, but it looked like sweat. It seems impossible, I know. That an old man crawled into a child's fort and died there. That the child said nothing to anyone. Was there a smell of decay, of decomposition, of rotting flesh? Not that I recall. Was there actually a dead man?

Memory tells me that I left a tea towel in the icebox for him to wipe his forehead. He needed *more* protection, I told him. So his eyes wouldn't get scorched, so the bald places wouldn't burn. I brought a dusty cowboy hat down from our attic and tucked the back behind the man's head, but the leather strap squeezed his fleshiness under the chin and made him look uncomfortable, as if he were choking. I returned it to the attic shelf in exchange for the Panama hat my father wore at the ocean on the rare summer daytrip. Crushed against the leaves at the old man's neck, the hat still looked magnificent. The light straw balanced his pallor. It had an elegant, wide black band and a brim to shade his thin eyelids from the sun. The addition of my father's sunglasses made the old man look smart, truly a tourist in my woods.

Over the new few days, I carried more things down to the fort. In a closet I found an old costume my mother had made for me, cottony wings and a halo made of tinfoil. I took the Panama hat off and wedged the silvery ring on the old man's head. I inserted the wings under the plywood behind his shoulders, tips bent up for shade. However, in the morning when I returned, all the fluff from the wings had been plucked off by a bird or squirrel wanting material for its nest. I removed the wing outlines, leaned them on the chrome trim, and put my father's straw hat back on the man's head. In this way, May wore into June and the end of school. Waiting for the raspberries to ripen, I continued to study the man. Something between us was starting to change.

After my last day at Green Marsh Elementary, my first day of summer vacation, my time in the woods was restricted. My father, wishing me to learn more cultured behaviors, took me daily across the bridge to restaurants, museums, boutiques in the Annapolis harbor. "Stand up straight," he instructed, smoking his pipe. While he worked, I sat behind a front desk and colored with crayons, avoiding mourners. "Chin up, hands out of your mouth." Even as I tried to obey, my father receded further. "Don't chew your lip. Did you clean under your nails?"

When I went out to the fort, I told the old man how my mother had loved the woods and how my father never spoke her name. I talked about issues of his comfort, my concerns, events of the day. The old man's face stayed expressionless and cold. I began to feel that something there was wrong. But surely he had his reasons for lying so silent. Maybe he was in pain. Maybe his ideas were too deep to put into words. Or he just wanted to be left alone. Or he needed something I couldn't provide. Wearing the Panama hat, he took on that last sort of look. With his pursed lips and shaded eyes, he looked like a man whom the world obeyed. Austere, powerful, as if waiting for public tribute. I wanted that look. I brought a mirror down to the fort and a shade hat my mother had worn gardening. I practiced with my face. Sometimes at dinner I shot the look at my father, who did not respond.

One Saturday, the old man watched indifferently as I fell from the double-trunked elm. I tripped to the spring, leg bleeding where the rusty milk-truck had scraped my leg. "Why don't you say something," I yelled. "The least you could do is be sorry it happened." Nothing. The orange-clay mouth was freezing cold as I knelt to wash the gash.

WHEN I WROTE TO MY FATHER about the Annapolis job offer, I received no letter back. I telephoned. It was the first time we had talked since my law degree. He was not well, he said. Lung cancer, stage four. It was terminal.

ONE SUNDAY MORNING mid-June of that summer I was eight, I decided my judgment had been wrong. The old man in my fort was not powerful, nor unfeeling; he was just sad and uncomfortable. The Panama hat, for one thing, bothered him. I took it off his head and placed it on his chest. From the field I cut Queen Anne's lace and cornflowers, arranging the flowers in the tin can. Under a shady birch I found some dog violet blossoms and put them on his eyes. I placed the cool shard of Indian pottery in his hand.

It was that evening while I shelled peas that my father announced we were moving across the bridge. I dropped the colander into the sink. "Dad, I don't want to move."

"Lucy, watch what you're doing."

I backed down the stepstool over to the table.

"What are you doing?" he said, not turning his head.

I walked out the kitchen door and into my woods. "Lucy," I heard my father calling from the backyard. I paid him no mind. It was dusk, and muggy, hot inside and out. I climbed over the fallen log and into the woods. When I reached the upturned roots of my fort, the first thing I saw was the shard of Indian pottery on the ground. Then the absence of the man's head. In place of his body under the plywood shelter, a raw bare spot. I scanned the ravine. No old man.

I searched everywhere. I found the Panama hat beside the spring, sitting on its top, open like a pot. Inside, a daddy longlegs crawled in the failing light. There was nothing to do but pick it up and return to the fort. I plucked raspberries and dropped them in the straw hat and cried.

It was a Tuesday after the Fourth of July beach traffic had subsided that we moved across the Bay Bridge. Our belongings preceded us. Our new house was in the historical district near the docks. When we reached Annapolis, we ate in a restaurant, and my father gave me a choice for the afternoon: go set up our new home, or come with him for a few hours to his office. I told my father I'd prefer neither of these. I'd prefer to walk around. In his dark suit, ponderously puffing his pipe, my father looked at me a long moment.

"Come on, then," he said.

We strode from the restaurant through the market, up Cornhill to State Circle. People parted and rushed. My father asked if I was wearing my watch. I nodded.

"At five o'clock," he said, "find this white oak. If you get lost, ask for the State House. Find this tree. Wait at that bench. I will come find you, be assured."

Coughing, he disappeared into the swarm of dark suits, and I set off on my own. When he was finished doing what he had to do, he came and found me, and we went home.

When we moved across the Bridge, he and I stopped cooking dinner. We went to restaurants for crab imperial, broiled rockfish, oysters on the half shell. My father dropped me off at a Massachusetts boarding school when I was twelve. I saw him at Christmas and for brief periods during summers. At one of my graduations, he appeared, dressed in the perpetual dark suit. For the rest, I received money in cards.

One summer during my college years, I went back to my woods, but the ravine wasn't the place I remembered. It was crowded between field and river, littered and erosion-scarred. The backyard was smaller, the house a different shape, the roads unfamiliar. It was like visiting my mother in Whitemarsh Cemetery and trying to find solace in a headstone, in granite-etched wings.

IT IS LATE September again. I am sitting on the State Circle bench. People mill around like so many falling leaves: momentous, private, discrete. In the hopper, there is a copy of a note my father wrote, politely refusing to arrange the memorial service for Walter Grinestaff. I do not know his reasons for turning down Fiona's request. Perhaps he hadn't given up hope that his architect friend might reappear, hearty and hale. My father left his pinky ring atop the hopper when he walked off, and it still fits my index finger. Every time I move my hand, it flashes in the sun, reminding me of the spring after the winter my mother died, the creek, the woods, my old man. The evening he went missing from my fort, there was a disturbance of ground, as if something hadn't wanted to let him go. I have a memory of tracks at the spring, of raccoons, where they washed their food, but what did I know of tracks? Were leaves dragged around, branches broken low? Maybe there were wild dogs, as my father always feared. But this I can't believe. I'd rather think the dead man shook the mites and cobwebs from his frame, climbed out of the fort through the ravine to the spring, entered the Choptank, and swam past Oystershell Point, past Cambridge Bridge, past Cook Point. To recover from the woods. To children who forgive him. To all there is to love in this world.

DRUNK

The Baby

OUR BEST lovemaking was on Sundays. Kerri and I started in the morning, me spooning eggs into her mouth, licking jam off her fingers, holding her in the kitchen, my body turning on from inside. Kerri, my wife, who was a nurse at Dorchester General, would give off this heat, and for the rest of the day she'd be unpredictable in her limbs, angelic but clumsy like a creature that could run, or swim, or fly away within hours. We'd been trying to make a baby for several years, and I'd been tested, and so had she. Our doctors said there was no reason we couldn't get pregnant, but we'd had no luck or maybe there was something the doctors couldn't diagnose, I didn't know. But on Sundays, I gave up worrying. It was like a stream, a tide, an understated song, punctuated by all the small accidents my lovely but clumsy wife would cause.

That June had been hotter than most, and we'd decided that particular morning to drive up from Easton and take the Bellevue Ferry over to Oxford to watch sailboats. Kerri drove, and I was touching her leg, painting from knee to thigh. I was thinking about an approaching deadline, a review I had to write for a beach reading special the *Star-Republican* was doing on love poetry. Every time I'd get up there, close to her center, the starting point, the well and source of it all, she'd sigh, and I'd lean and kiss her neck. I wanted to talk about poetry, the cat and last gods of Galway Kinnell. I pulled out the book. Green fields lined the road on both sides. I read ten sonnets and then reached the eleventh, "Lips blowsy from kissing," when Kerri slowly and absentmindedly drove off the edge of the road. A sea of soybean leaves surrounded our car. "That's okay," I said, and she said, "Oh Kevin, I hope you'll always be able to say that," and she backed out of the field.

We missed the exit, drove all the way to St. Michael's, and Kerri turned the car around. We found the turn-off to Bellevue and entered a lot down by the ferry. As she parked, my wife knocked into a polished white Jag, our cars bumping only lightly, but it was enough to trigger the Jag's alarm. That was our life's pattern. Soft and slow, harmony between us, and then a car alarm. What could I do? I cupped my wife's chin until she started to smile. I said, "Don't worry about it," and I laughed, and she laughed, and we disappeared into the sound.

On the ferry dock, we watched the Tred Avon sparkle in the sun. The morning had broken into a hundred desires, small pieces I picked up like cards. I loved to watch Kerri's face when she was in that state. Her eyes glittered like fish jumping out of the water. We ferried across and ate crab cakes at the Robert Morris Inn. Then I drove, and we reached the marina and parked on the edge of someone's lawn. I walked over to open the passenger side door, and Kerri beat me to it, jumping out of the car. As she flung her purse over her shoulder, she accidentally released the straps. The purse slung backwards onto the sidewalk, seeming to explode once in the air and a second time on the road.

A little boy flying by on a bicycle squealed his brakes in surprise. He watched us and then came back and helped gather things up. Lipstick, keys, wallet, powder, all the contents of a wife's purse. Coins, hard candies, yellow ear plugs, torn pocket calendar, and a blue and white flat plastic container I had never seen before.

"What is that?" I asked.

Kerri looked vaguely at the little boy and thanked him, smiling in a not-so-real way she had.

I said again, "What's that plastic thing?"

"Oh that," she said. She handed a dollar to the boy, and then a wrapped-up butterscotch candy. "Well, pills, Kevin, you know, pills."

When you know someone like we knew each other then, eight years running, the last few full of trying and hoping and waiting, each person's face says things, wordless things, things deeper than understanding. Kerri waited for me to say like always, "Don't worry," but I turned away, and she had to shoulder her purse and follow. At the marina, I stared at the murky water and the pleasure boats. My wife was not good at being blamed, did not do grudges or feeling bad. My wife was made to commit small accidents, to be carefree, to laugh. She wouldn't be able to contain new life, and I should have known, eight years together. I'd hoped for a wife and a child, but instead, I had only a wife who wanted to make love on Sundays. Suddenly I felt that I'd lived a long time alone.

Kerri followed me along docks and bulwarks. Back on the streets we passed the boatyard, the old store, the mural of men dredging oysters. We walked to the other side of Oxford, the Tred Avon River nudging the shore at the town park, washing over submerged rocks, and gradually I cooled. I took my wife's hand and held it up to my mouth. Out on the river the wind filled boats' sails. Not looking at her face, I nibbled her fingers. Gulls laughed over the breeze. A little bit, a little bite like a fish on bait.

We drove back to our condo in Easton and lay on the sofa. Our take-out dinner sat on the coffee table, coconut rice noodles and duck braised in plum. In the morning, Kerri would return to the hospital, and I'd try to write. I thought about reading more sonnets aloud, but my heart wasn't in it. Shifting to get comfortable, my wife kicked over her wine glass. It emptied its belly onto the coffee table, red wine wrapping the stem of my glass. I kissed her toes and said, "Okay," and Kerri sighed like a sad child. Her wine glass was empty, mine half full, and her foot felt so small in my palm.

Cave

THE MOMENT IT HAPPENED, Brian looked up into her eyes.

His most faithful parishioner stood before him, Mrs. Thornton, raw and soft, bland as potato flesh. Imagine a girl's cottony skin splashed and the strange, hot shame. A bit closer to your priest now? Say it to her, Father Brian Matthews, a bloody bit closer, now that she might imagine what you once did to a girl's sheets.

Just as he had felt then, embarrassed, the redness on the white ocean of sheets and Michelle McCready's body an expanse of softness, then bloodied, opened and bleeding on the sheets, the vision was like driving, he remembered it well, the year of the Beatles playing in his father's car late at night, headed to Michelle McCready's place when her parents were away, having left for their vacation in the mountains for one blessed week, knowing that Michelle Mc-Cready would welcome him and treat him badly both at the same time, tease him about being a prude and devout and still a virgin at late eighteen, both of them getting out of Cambridge, heading off in the fall, Brian on the edge of something greater than himself, knowing that if he should jerk the wheel in a fit that would be yes, uncontrolled, uncontrollable and desired, the car would speed at seventy miles per hour so powerfully into the trees lining the road that all of his body would hurl forward, fly forth into the black pitch of glass and headlights and noise and blood and maybe fire. Brian had trembled and his hands shook. He regained control, slowly, over his erection, anchored, bobbing there like temptation but not sin.

The white altar cloth was set and adorned. Mrs. Thornton, near retirement from North Cambridge High, wavered at its side. There were the two candles, lit, the presence of Christ. The book opened to the Eucharistic prayers. The golden plate piled with small communion disks and on top, one unbroken wafer. Two cruets holding wine and water to mix. The silver chalice. Charlie Connolly, the altar boy, elfish and cherubic, wobbling over in sneakers under his white tunic. Pouring a splash of water, innocent as a spigot. Proffering the pure white towel on his arm.

"Lord, cleanse me of my iniquity, wash me from my sin," Father Matthew murmured, turning from Charlie to the altar. His voice rose like a bell. "Brothers and sisters, pray the Lord accept our sacrifice."

Mrs. Thornton, Eucharistic minister at St. Andrew's, swayed by the altar. She had known Father Brian Matthews since he was Charlie's age, accepting every flaw and glory as bumps in the road.

Her eyes watered, blue, lined with pink and white, swollen like clouds, mildly serene, not splashed with blood or wine or a bit of guilt as they entered the inner sanctum, the vibration, the repetition, the miracle over and over again in the vault of the church— mystery flooded Brian's body, holy, holy, holy, the enormous song rising like dense fog, lifting up that night he'd driven out to the house of Michelle McCready, the ritual words, dancing with an unseen partner, thousands of years of circling, then a stumble.

The partner stumbled, or he stumbled?

This is the body and blood, he was saying to Mrs. Thornton, who waited for the kiss of afterlife, so close to her lips, but as her tongue approached for the body, the sip of blood, he tripped. On his alb? A misstep on his chasuble? Why this morning should the universe hiccup and he stumble? Mrs. Thornton did not want this, to be thrown by this slip like an old mare on a rabbit hole. Think fast now, Father Matthews. Think control. Grab the wheel. Don't laugh, don't cry, stay on the road. Look at Charlie, he's just a child. Tell him to hurry to the sacristy, grab a white towel, three or four or seven, even. *Go Charlie.* Who does, sneakers twisting past the altar. *Shh, you're okay.* You have your period? Lord, help me, I'm stained. She's a pool, deep, deep and soft, and I'm a boy, pink cheeked, unbearded. Meteors crashed into planets, Copernicus routed Ptolemy, a baseball once shattered Mrs. Thornton's window leading to Brian's first lie, and Michelle McCready bled like death his first and last time. *Mrs. Thornton, hold this corner*, still white, not wet here. Hold it so the blood doesn't spill on the floor. Please God, let her stop bleeding, forgive me my sins, oh Mrs. Thornton, say it, Brian Matthews, come back in time now, *May this sacrifice bring us to everlasting life*, but still he sees the redness everywhere, on the altar, the white table, spilling over the plate of consecrated host.

Rorschach Test

GRAPES, sieve, feather boa.

In a hotel room in New York, New York, I, Mindy Wright, brunched on poached eggs and trout and French wine. I realized I might have drunk too much when, walking over the thick beige carpet, it was like I'd mounted a seesaw, a grown-up perched on the other side. I picked up each foot and put it down with care, how I used to walk through parties in high school, when I'd just discovered drunkenness, speed and bump, the seesaw, how to place my foot lightly until the down goes up, nudging through groping and music until you reached the hallway where girls stood to wait for the bathroom, and you fell into line.

Feather boa, breasts, basket.

But it was not the wine, exactly, my head had been tilting before. After high school, and then college, having dropped into the blank of a real world, I was glad to know something finally: that solitude was the answer to life. The world seemed more manageable up there in the hotel room, I felt larger and more powerful. I leaned back on the bed frame until my head touched the wall, and I drank more of the expensive wine.

Basket, eyelashes, sea.

Ever since graduation from Salisbury University, disappointing my mother who'd planned for the Ivy Leagues, I'd been traveling around the country. My favorite English professor, Tim Rhodes, had given me a poetry collection called *When One Has Lived a*

Long Time Alone, and that was the book I carried. I loved the berry, the swallow, the great maternal pine. My mother had quit sending money in March when I turned twenty-two, so I stopped and stayed for free wherever I found friends. I'd been hoping to escape from something, maybe into those poems.

Sea, man's hand, drum.

That week, I'd hit the jackpot. I'd been in Boston for a couple weeks with some old North Cambridge friends when my mother called to tell me that Uncle Ron, her sister's husband, was attending a convention in NYC. He was an economics professor at Stanford, and I could stay for free at his fancy hotel until Monday. A free room on Times Square was a great free room, and Mom said my uncle was a very smart man.

Drum, lace, pumping heart.

He picked me up that Thursday at Penn Station in his rental car, a red convertible. Tracy Chapman sang on the radio, and I was thinking nothing when he put his hand on mine and yelled, "Hey Mindy," over the music. "Why don't you call me Ronald so my colleagues don't ask questions?" I yelled back, "Okay, Uncle Ron," laughing, turning my head to look at oncoming cars. It was the first day of his convention. He kept his hand on mine as he drove.

Pumping heart, cat, eggs.

Then he squeezed my hand, and I hoped we'd veer into traffic, a city bus, head-on, smash, economist and me and all. Had Uncle Ron forgotten I was his wife's niece? That night, he took me to a restaurant overlooking the Hudson and we ate lobster. It took careful observation for me to convince myself it was not lust, just loneliness at being away from my aunt. On Friday, he took me to

MoMA, teaching me about the economics of art, and later, to a Broadway play. Saturday, he attended the convention all day, and I wandered around Central Park, and we met for dinner in Soho.

Eggs, tinsel, tongue.

I didn't really like poached eggs and trout. My wine glass matched the two from the previous night's champagne, when my uncle held my waist and stared too long in my eyes. In the morning, he pushed the hotel beds close while I was taking a bath, and said, "Why don't you order room service while I go to my last meeting? I'll be back at two this afternoon." Outside the window, the sun shone brightly over the city, and the light pushing through the thin curtain made shapes in a shadow show, which, most of the morning, I watched.

Tongue, single wing, grapes.

Thoughts can fill immensity. I, Mindy Wright, spilled wine all over the beige carpet while trying to decide whether to stay or to run. Refilling my glass, I kept chanting a phrase that had struck me, one I've remembered for the rest of my life: it's the patterns that matter, the patterns that matter, not content, but content in form. I stopped worrying about the wine blotch on beige. It was just a crazy Sunday morning, one more in a line, and I left, dear Reader, before he returned.

A Perdurable Life

CATFISH, pickerel, perch, croaker, shiner, bass: when a fish came out of the Choptank, it would thrash like my first cat did when Father ran her over with the tractor. I had to hold tightly or the rod would fly out of my hands, heavy and twitching. Father would say, "Hang on!" I never wanted to touch a fish hanging on its line. Someone snapped a photo of me when I was five or six, holding up a string of catfish at the farm, probably Mother who rode along to take in sun. Father is wearing a bleached hat, and I stand beside him on our Boston Whaler, worrying about the fishes' sharp fins, my chubby long face a study in lament. I remember believing that if a dead fish touched me I might die.

I never dreamed of sleeping with anyone before I married. The only person who ever kissed me was Father. Mother would scold him, "You spoil the child." Long before I met my husband, I went on one date. A heavy, shy boy had invited me to the Spring Ball at Catholic University but he spent the whole dance talking to his friends. I was twenty years old. My roommate Brenda kept me company afterward as I cried and cuddled my twin cats. A decade later, at thirty, I had never been kissed. The night before my wedding, I lay in a hotel bed, nervous as death.

DISCARD, sequence, stock, hearts, spades, knock: words are easy to come by, good for pushing out thoughts. On my wedding night, Sister Paul, a good friend of our family, lay in the twin bed across the room. She was a huge mound breathing so heavily I thought something must be wrong. My legs clenched like joints on a boat. Sister Paul used to go with Father and Mother and me from Washington, D.C. down to the Dorchester County farm. We played gin rummy and double solitaire. I wanted to be a nun, too, ordered and plump and as clear as cards, but Sister Paul's convent had rejected me. Our hours of cards, quiet and communal, led to this pre-wedding dawn. I wiped my face on my pillow and pretended that warm, down thing was a husband. At seventy, Sister Paul was the person who'd pointed out my big catch.

"Your future husband," she'd said. "He's a teacher." Every spring, Holy Redeemer's in Bethesda threw a dance to thank all the teachers and volunteers, and that's where Sister Paul and the pastor had planned to have us meet, always a fine affair, except that the previous May, the organist had had a stroke on the dance floor. I'd cried for days. Mother said, "Cut the self-pity." This year, a twang of sadness struck when the pastor remembered the dead woman in prayer. Then Sister Paul bumped into someone on purpose, pulling me along like a door prize.

"Ed Bailey, meet my sweet young friend June Remington," she said. We stood at the punch bowl eating cubes of cheese. I wished I could disappear into Sister's large embrace, but she waddled off.

"I'm a math teacher at the middle school," Ed said. "Yes," I mumbled. My palms were wet. He asked, "You count the offering after mass?" I said, "Yes." He said, "Do you like the Platters? I don't dance, but the Platters—" The music crashed in the middle of its tune. People gasped and someone cried, "Heart attack!" Ed Bailey didn't even look at me, just bolted up to the stage. I stood on a chair to see. He pushed away the crowd, bent down, and gave someone mouth-to-mouth.

TRUMPETS, trombones, sax, piano, guitars, drums: the ten-piece band had been reduced by one, and we all looked on in shock. My face crumbled. I couldn't help but cry. The pastor called off the dance, and Sister escorted me to the door. Next day, Ed Bailey telephoned my apartment and said the musician had died. "There's little chance of success with CPR, less than five percent," Ed said, "but I got to practice for the next time." I didn't know what to say. "I got tickets to the Platters," Ed said. "Would you go?" That was the last thank-you dance. Next May in its place, Ed and I got married. Mother gave Father what-for, allowing a teacher named Ed Bailey to wed a Remington. When we posed at the altar, she kissed me on the cheek, and it felt like she had a marble in her mouth. I was crying again. Mother whispered, "Quit your faking."

There is a black and white photograph of us on the church lawn. Father's cheeks are puffed proud and Mother's are a drawn purse. My husband looks like a fishing pole. I am belly-white. I was so exhausted after the wedding. We left for our honeymoon to Niagara Falls, and we were back again before I truly awoke.

AMBROSE, Jade, Rump, Finky, Inga, Bett: before marriage, I had kept twin cats, three parakeets, and a spider monkey released from the University of Maryland science lab. Bett, the monkey, had a bad temper that made her bite and hurl poop. Ed, who was very good at taking care of humans, didn't believe in letting animals in the house. Though I don't remember our honeymoon, during it I'd managed to convince Ed that parakeets didn't shed or smell. We brought the birds to our new house in the D.C. suburbs, and my old college roommate Brenda took my other pets.

Nine months after our honeymoon, I gave birth to my daughter. I named her Kitty, in honor of the cats. Mother sent a maid to help with the baby, and two days after the doctors let me bring Kitty home, that maid slipped on a step and dropped her. My daughter lay like something dead. I chuffed down the twenty-eight stairs, heart blown wide open, and leaned forward, shaking, to touch her mouth. It emitted a cat-pitched howl. All the way to Sibley Memorial Hospital that mewling continued, and I couldn't bear to touch her. Ed had to both drive and hold the baby. The hospital x-ray showed a crack in the skull. The doctor said, "Don't worry, everything will be okay." I cradled and pet my daughter and wanted to break that maid's neck. I was afraid Kitty would be brain-damaged, but she spoke words before she could even sit up. By two, she could almost read. Ed was proud, but I felt sad. What good were babies who grew up so fast?

I got pregnant again and along came our first son, Corey. Kitty taught her brother everything she knew. Corey taught his sister to laugh. One day, my old roommate sat across the table from me and said I looked tired. Kitty zoomed through the kitchen pulling Corey's hand. "I've been taking classes in massage," Brenda said. "Let me practice on you." "No—" I said. "It'll take the sad out of your back," she said. When Brenda's fingers touched my shoulder, it was already too much. She asked, "Is this okay?" I stared at my hands. I tried to ask if she saw my kids but her hands were all thumbs pushing hard and I couldn't speak. My mouth tightened like a fish line. "That okay?" she asked. Too much pushing, I tried to say. I wanted to twist away. "Kitty," I shrieked, "come here." The next time Brenda offered a massage, I had an excuse. "Nothing strenuous," I told her. "I'm pregnant again." Nine months later, Jay Rocky Remington was born. Ed and I decided to move away from the D.C. suburbs down to the Eastern Shore.

HEMLOCK, maple, oak, wheat, beans, corn: Ed negotiated with Father and bought two acres of my parents' riverfront farm. He found a job teaching math in Cambridge, the nearest town. Kitty said, "Third grade's good for a new start." Corey begged for an outdoor dog. I cradled baby J.R. and looked out the window at the Choptank. In various directions, I saw endless trees, fields, and marsh. I was embarrassed to be sad on the farm and only cried when I was alone with the baby and the new dog.

Our first fall in Dorchester County, I stood in the kitchen, weepy, whispering to the baby, "It's not that Mommy doesn't love you," when our dog came to the porch to bark. I went to hush him. That's when he lunged at a brown mound in the drying corn. Setting J.R. down on the lawn, I walked to the edge of the field and leaned in to see. Among the stalks was a river otter, its back bent in half. One leg was chewed away, fur mashed down in blood, and one eye leaked, split by our dog. Its other eye looked at me, milky, clouding. When I knelt down, that dead otter thrashed.

I sucked in my breath, scooped up the baby, kicked at the dog, and ran across the lawn. I shut us in my room, lying on the bed and clutching the baby to my chest. I telephoned my parents but could only gasp when Mother answered the phone. I called Green Marsh Middle and asked for Ed. When he got to the phone, he asked, "What is it?" A hook pinched my throat. "Things are dying," I said, and Ed said, "I'll be right home." He picked the lock on our bedroom door. Holding J.R. on his lap, Ed drove toward Dorchester General while I cried and dry-heaved and slumped on the passenger door. In the emergency room, the doctor gave me a shot. I spent the next week sleeping before it got so I could talk. The doctor, a psychologist, asked, "What are you afraid of?" I thought of dead things twitching and felt my stomach turn. "What?" the doctor asked. "Dying," I said. Ed, soft like a worn towel, visited. Mother offered to send him a maid to run the house, but Ed said he would figure it out.

He telephoned Sister Paul at her retirement convent. Would she come up from Florida for a visit? Old as she was, Sister said yes. After she arrived, Kitty and Corey wrote me letters. Corey wrote, "It's okay, Mom, come home." Kitty's letter said, "It's too boring around here without you." I told the doctor about these letters, and that I feared my kids were dying. "What do you mean?" asked the doctor. "Kitty's finishing third grade," I said. Otter, heron, muskrat, pintail, redwing, coon: I told him one of my lists. He made notes and asked, "What upsets you most?" I said, "I'm sad." The doctor agreed, and asked, "Are you a good mother?" I thought about it a long while. I thought of Mother and Father. I thought about myself. I don't know if I found an answer, but eventually I felt ready to go home.

It was a school night, and my house smelled of detergent and bleach. Kitty stood by the kitchen sink. "She's a good girl," Sister Paul said. Baby J.R., looking older, hugged my arm. Corey announced he'd learned some card games. He dealt and we played. Ed came home from work with a pile of cats, saying, "They're neutered." Kitty took a black kitten up to her room. Corey said he'd stick to cards. J.R. squealed and grabbed a gray one by the tail, and we named it Catfish.

CORN, tomatoes, crabs, oysters, snowdrift, eggs: despite the impermanence of everything, I learned to keep my poise, raising chickens and pickling vegetables and attending school plays. Kitty got an after-school job at the hospital. Corey studied magic. J.R. wanted to be a waterman. When Ed and I got word from Florida that Sister Paul was failing, we decided to take the kids on a trip. Kitty asked time off from her job, Corey practiced card tricks in the car, and J.R. brought his wading boots. Entering Sister Paul's room, they all hung behind my skirt.

When Sister spoke, she wheezed. Black whiskers straggled out of her chin. "Tomorrow," she gasped, "the caretaker can take them out to fish." Ed took the children to look for Spanish moss while I sat with Sister Paul. Her breath mixed with the drip of a courtyard fountain. Outside, my children shouted. "Look," I heard my daughter exclaim, "bulgy eyes." Corey called, "Ooh, that one's dead."

J.R. shouted, "No way." Their voices flew through the open windows. Ed called, "Come here, they won't hurt you." Sister's mouth wrinkled, and her blue irises swam, and her face was squeezed tight by the black and white cloth. She flopped out her arm, and her hand reached for me. "You're a good girl," she heaved.

Listing my family over and over in my head, I took Sister's hand and held it away from my body, feeling five or six, my big head wanting Father to take it away. I should have smoothed her loose gray strands behind her wimple, but it was all I could do to hold steady. Then I heard J.R. say, "Daddy, let me!" My family trooped into the room carrying tiny luminescent frogs. J.R. cupped the frog for us to feel, and Sister released my hand. J.R. whispered, awestruck, "Their feet can grip the trees."

I followed the children outside. Kitty and Corey ran their fingers through the hanging moss, and J.R. waded through the trees. A few yards away, at the blue ocean's edge, the caretaker washed out his Boston Whaler. J.R. waved at the inlet and shouted, "Mommy, we're going out there tomorrow?" Ed asked the caretaker to take our picture, and we clambered into the boat. "Are you having fun?" the caretaker asked. Ed clasped my hand and we posed. It was a bright day. In this photo, hanging among all the others on my refrigerator, we are breathless, the children gripping the sides of the boat, their father and me, each other. Aboard the parked boat, my family gleams. Above and before us, the trees teem with frogs. This picture lives next to the one of me with the line of fish, next to a matching one of J.R., when he was five or six, head too large for his body, holding a big catfish on a line. On his face, a wide smile. Now he's almost grown, and he's sleeping with his girlfriend, which I know because when he returns to his college in Salisbury, I clean his room.

PANTIES, stockings, brush, barrette, t-shirt, bra: some habits don't change. I pretend they belong to my daughter. Holidays when Kitty visits from her medical school on the other side of the country, she'll come downstairs holding someone else's private item, asking, "What's this?" For a second I have no idea. Then I remember putting it in her room, over her chair, in her drawer. "Does it belong to one of your friends?" I say, praying she will agree for once. My daughter nods slowly and smiles.

Words That Bend Toward Love

When the cancer first pinched, Doc fought with all his salt. The crab clamped and twisted its poisoned claw while he looked for a cure-all and tried to keep back the voice that says *time up* but it crawled off the sickroom's chandelier and lintel and hearth down the grand stairs and halls through lawns and orchards and horse fields to the marsh. Doc abandoned his senses near eight weeks back. Sometimes it's drink he wants and other times it's prayer. Doc Fossett has more faith than I'll ever know. The rest of the time he calls for his son.

Such as when I'm tucking the big white napkin under his chin and he says to me, "William!"

His son William disappeared near two years back. I step back and bury my left hand in my apron.

"O Helen," he says. "Helen where's my son?"

"I don't rightly know sir," I say.

I settle the dinner tray on his lap thinking how his crazy daughter is all he's got now. Her and me. Doc bought this Tuckahoe estate three decades ago and it included Nathan's and my house.

Doc's wife wanted to turn us away but Doc hired us for farm and domestic help. About two years later she left complaining of mosquitoes and poison ivy and since that day I've managed the house and my husband Nathan the land. When the Doc leaves everything to his children we plan to keep on just so.

After dinner the overnight nurse throws her bags on the good chair and I exit through the back door for my nightly walk. The driveway pebbles under my feet. My husband waits on the stoop of our whitewashed cabin. He sits on the stoop watching me with his good eye.

"Hullo Helen," he says. "You're home."

I nod and head over to a wicker basket on our lawn. Sticking clothespins in my mouth I take our underclothes off the line. I fold them carefully over my basket. Tuck them into shapes gently. Wrinkled things being laid down. Nathan comes and holds me under the linens. We walk to the marshy cove to sit on the dock our little Samuel built. Nathan massages my tired right hand and my crippled left one. He's gentle around the stumps.

He says, "It's a pretty night."

I lay my head on his neck and breathe in skin. The moon shows broken through the trees. Two tame ducks swim up and beak my foot. I say, "Old man is close near dead."

THE NIGHT NURSE doesn't clean so this morning I run water over gravy that's hardened up. Those pale blue eyes and that big brain are failing him. I hum into the dishwater *old man is close near dead*. I fish out a blue and white dinner plate. Last night after the Doctor called me William I watched him with his hand trembling like a horse lip as he forked and dropped his bite. William's long gone and the old man knows well as I. The boy ran his reckless self away from the mansion house.

I slip piece after piece of china into the sink. The Doctor's entire set. Sometimes I imagine his son William belly-up and wrapped in a sail. Sometimes I remember him a teenager cussing out me and his little sister Teresa. Mostly I see him a baby crawling from my lap across the kitchen floor toward my grandson Samuel.

Doc Fossett looks round his bedstead to where I stand at the door with his tray of breakfast. Maybe he sees a fishhook floating through the room. Maybe a halo not a hook. Out of breath. "It's the –n–," he mumbles to me.

"No sir not yet."

"—d," he says. I pour some coffee steaming black and step into the corner to watch awhile. The Doctor has staved off fear a long time. He halves end into pieces. The *en* and *d*. The *e* and *nd*. Makes shapes of the letters.

"Calm yourself," I say.

Pain gets the Doctor. He is on the rack with the crab cramping his liver. The river is close. Maybe the spirits will carry him. Spirit him away to the Church that takes his money. He feels drafts passing through the room. He says things aloud. Bits of this and that stuffed and stashed. He says *ivory cane*. He gets a roaming cool. A chill like the one traveling his spine. *Diamond pin*, he says. Maybe he senses there beside him a formless form. Sometimes he says *gold crucifix*. Light glint and nailed hands and thorny crown. *Jesus* he says with the toast crumbs dribbling down. "Where is my son?"

I bite my tongue.

He says, "I'm not ready for the e—."

AFTER CLEARING BREAKFAST I check on my girl. Teresa is too old to say girl but no one would call her a woman. She's kneeling by her canopied four-poster bed. I whisper, "Honey your father drawing close to his reward."

She looks up and makes the sign of the cross.

At the sink I pick dried egg off the blue peacock who hides somewhere on every piece of china. The dishwater splashes. I sink into the soap. The girl is crazy and what does Doc care? Old man's reward is coming to slouch next to him and tickle his chin. William is the one he coddled. The boy escaped Talbot County to go to college in Virginia and he faded farther south to study law. Moved to Key West right when Doc Fossett fell sick. Vanished like a ghost with a load of the Doctor's cash. Maybe he stepped off the last of those Keys and opened up the ocean.

I lift the oval platter to rub at a chipped edge. The water drips off my elbow. Something out the window catches my eye. Teresa in a white shawl wanders around the backyard. Under the maple tree she talks to herself and swings her rosary beads. All that girl's love turned into religion. Old man doesn't know his right hand from his left.

When Doc is dead Nathan and I are moving into the downstairs to help out Teresa. We deserve it. Doctor's been whining about *tribulation* and *last rites* and I've tried and told him to settle himself but I want to say something else. *You do remember sir how I lost these fingers with the kitchen knife* I want to say. *Chopped my third off here and my fourth at the knuckle? The same year a combine tossed a rock into Nathan's eye?* I pick up a teacup with peonies and bluebells and ivy and peacock hidden on the side.

Before the old man dies I do plan to tell him about Samuel.

THE BELL RINGS from upstairs. It is lunchtime and Doc will be ordering his coffee with an extra drop because some habits die hard. He claims he never was a drinker. Just a couple shots a night, maybe four or six when the good old boys came down from Baltimore to his country estate, or when the priests from St. Andrew's dropped by. The cancer started in his liver. When I refuse to pour his drink he'll be all fury and bile.

In bed the doctor is shaking his wrist and putting up an imaginary watch to his ear. I do feel some affection for the old man. Life is too short. *Leather strap* he says to himself and I see him hearing the voice that whispers *time up.* I settle my crooked smile and place his tray on the stand.

His wheels turn. "Take this away and send in my son!" he roars.

Doc wants to wipe away that clawing in his gut.

"O yes," he says.

His boy knows how to sail and they'll take a trip like they used to, a cruise to the islands like before William disappeared. I head toward the door.

"Wait Helen where's my son?"

He made the boy's fortune so why isn't William here now at the e–d? Not like his good daughter. "Physician heal thyself," I mutter.

He stares at me standing in the doorway and sees I've got more to say. What is it?

"Sir you remember my grandson Samuel?" I am unable to say

the truth so I tell a different story. "He had a pet rabbit that took fright. Must've heard a hawk flying over. Did you know a rabbit tied down can break its back?"

He says, "Helen just bring me a pint of ale."

Back in medical school Doc and the boys drank till their eyes were glass. He thinks he'll make it through this cancer. If he stays calm as calm all his offerings might suffice. But I say all that money and brains are good for nothing now. I hope he remembers to call in Teresa before he dies.

When the crab whispers in his head again Doc clutches his sheets with an image sprung into his eye. What is it? The bank of the river. A boat. A rod. A rusty hook. He presses his brow. *Why'd I send off my boy* he's thinking. *To cast his wild bait?* He's wishing William would take him down to the river to the boat. *To cash in his oats?* The trusty wooden boat.

"Helen O Helen where is my son?" he moans.

Before leaving the doorframe I try again to talk straight and loud right at him.

I say, "Old man you don't know Helen."

I DON'T HEAR another peep until I return to clear the plates.

Somewhere in his mind he's thinking I mouthed *old man you don't know hell*. But I didn't say that. I spoke up but I didn't say that. He expects *go to hell*. I heard him screaming on the phone the night his own old man died. He said, "I made my own million, don't need your money, so you go to hell." Knows that phrase. He yelled it at his father on his deathbed. Thinks it again and again now on his bed. *You go to hell*. Thinks he's young again and drink up boys! It's how you run the thing. Drive a hard bargain and buy out the old men. Buy up the land. We'll be millionaires before we're thirty. *Time up* the voice says now and Doc hollers, "Go to hell!"

Clutches his abdomen in pain and turns his head.

"William come home," he sobs.

From her room Teresa hears him ranting and kneels down. Her eyes are dry from years of prayer.

I WONDER about the life I've hidden from him. Why now with the Doctor sick does it want to spill out so bad? How my mama died? So tired she slept through a fire in a whitewashed shack and the soles burned off her feet. She never could walk right again. Maybe I'm like mama wanting to ease the pain. I want to tell Doc Fossett what he doesn't know about my son Tommy. Whose wife slipped when she was pregnant and mopping the floor. How she raced to the hospital but the doctors wouldn't see her quick enough. How after the baby died and she left, my Tommy worked himself to death.

Plates are dirty again from lunch. On the platter there's a butterfly floating next to a sweet pea next to a peacock. I dip the platter in the water. The bird's tail feathers drip and his beak is open.

A sudden gust pillows the kitchen curtain. Barefoot and draped in white Teresa kneels under the weeping cherry. I step back holding the platter and feeling things bubble up on my inside. Butterfly. Sweet pea. Peacock. I throw the platter onto the kitchen floor. The plate and the saucer and the teacup shatter blue and white on the tile.

I IMAGINE Doc Fossett up in his room wondering what this din is. Is someone rummaging in his pockets? Is Saint Peter clanging his keys? Are hellhounds gnashing at their bowls? *It's me* I want to say and I want to say more.

When I climb the stairs to the sickroom my knees feel so old. I stop at the landing. The sun heats the window glass. The roof needs repair. The estate stretches before me. The weeping cherry, the bottoms of Teresa's feet. I hold two pieces of china and I give myself a cut.

Catching my breath on the landing I hear Doc roar as loud as he is able, "Go to hell!"

My hand with only three fingers is red with blood. *I've got to tell you before you go sir. Never told you how my daughter Francine got pregnant when she was thirteen and bore my Samuel and she died but Samuel was alive. The boy we raised. My grandson Samuel remember him Doc? Nathan's and my joy?*

I climb the rest of the stairs.

"It's Helen sir," I say. "I came to tell you I broke this plate."

I hold up blue and white shards for him to see. I press my hand to a napkin to stem the blood. Doc's bed is trembling. He fingers his gold ring. Fingers point from the wallpaper. Rusty fishhooks haunt his bedroom. Here the bend in the road. The last fending. Bedding in head. Doc is livid and confused. "Who's this? Did I call? I'll take a whisky."

I breathe in and say, "Something else too."

"My son?" he moans.

"I've taken care of your family," I say. I breathe so deep I feel something snap. "But you don't know about mine."

Doc Fossett writhes in pain. Bells and alarms fill his head. There is something behind my eyes. When his son gets here and carries this bed down to the river he will escape. He will go for a dip. It isn't too late! But the crab's voice says *time up* and a form floats toward him, breath cold on his neck. "Where is William!"

"Samuel!" I wail back. "Do you know where he is?"

I think he hears my words.

"My grandson," I say, "the carpenter who worked on your shingles last fall."

I wave broken china toward the bay window and the roof. Does he see my bleeding left hand?

"The one who fell from the roof," I say.

Why why why is this girl waving he's wondering. The Doctor's eyes turn back into his head.

"Well he's dead."

IN HIS HEAD there is a flash. The boat and drinking like a fish in the river. There his wife driving off from the mansion and mosquitoes and marsh and children. There his son waving from the sailboat with an island girl on his lap. There his daughter lying in bed with a string of Our Fathers and Hail Marys on her breast. I am clutching pieces of blue and white with blood on my hand. The old man's eyes are wild. Beads of sweat on his crown.

I draw in my breath at the sight outside the bay window. Before me on the uneven shingles a row of doves nestle and coo in the sun.

"Where is she?" he gasps. "Where's my daughter?"

"Outside praying for you," I say. "It's her habit." I stop. I don't go.

And so my last word *habit* takes hold of the old man like fascination. It's been planning to come no matter the meaning of e-n-d he picks. He's not going to the river. The catch is over and no fish to be had. The form floating toward him solidifies into a white thing. Sheer transparent flesh. A body shimmering like water. Whiter than cloud. Faith in a boat. Doc will take an outing.

I put down the broken platter pieces and reach to hold his hands. The river is flying through the curtained window and flushes away the shards. The shooting sharp breath. The china in his heart.

His hands are soft and dry and then they are cold.

Sanderlings

"How you doing?" I ask.

"Not bad Cath," Patsy says.

"Need to use the ladies'?"

My sister nods, her hand warm in mine. Her eyes crinkle almost closed with the curl of her chapped lips as we enter the restroom, tiled and scented of lemon cleaner and sunscreen. You used to pay a dime to use the Ocean City public toilets, but now they're free. In a loud monotone, my sister reads the sign that says *Please do not flush sanitary products*. She went through menopause before me. Her doctor says all Down syndrome bodies age ten to twenty years faster than ours. She takes a long time in the stall.

"Okay in there?" I ask.

"Sure Cath."

A barefoot kid, nine or ten, stops to stare.

Patsy calls, "Don't you have to go?"

"I was right beside you." I finish drying my hands at the air blower. "Be right outside, okay?"

"Sure Cath."

On the payphone by the water fountain I call our father's house and hope to get my brother. But Dad answers, his voice dry. I picture him on the hospice bed, skin translucent like a shell, and I can't bring myself to speak.

"You two—having fun?" he manages.

"Dad, where's Fred?"

"Right here—want him?"

"No," I say, "I just wanted to let you know that we made it."

Dad says, "Tell Patsy—I love her."

I hang up. My sister toddles from the bathroom.

"Okay," she shouts.

She loves Ocean City, so I think it's the best place for us to have this talk about Dad.

"You ready?" I ask.

"Ready like Freddy," she says, and I wonder if she ever feels old.

I TEACH HISTORY at North Cambridge High School, where the students describe me as old. I got divorced when I was thirty-seven, we had no kids, and up until the past summer, I lived alone. My hips are round, my hair brown with patches of gray. My sister Patsy, overweight and the height of a child, lived with our father until he got too sick to take care of her, and now she lives with me. Patsy's head flattens out on the back. She goes to a vocational workshop in Cambridge and wears hearing aids in both ears.

For the car ride I gave her a coloring book on *Ancient Egypt*, which promised *Animals at play, gods and goddesses at sport, Egyptians at work*. Through Salisbury and down into the Wicomico countryside, she colored while Roger Miller sang *Ya can't roller skate in a buffalo herd.* I drove. Patsy colored and hummed through the long stretches of chicken-houses and soybeans. *Ya can't drive around with a tiger in your car*, Roger sang. By the time we got to the Route 50 Bridge, we'd listened to twenty-five familiar songs. Cleopatra blushed brick-red under turquoise stars. The Sphinx sat mahogany in sea-green sand.

"Nice work," I told her in the inlet parking lot.

"Thanks Cath," she said. "Thanks."

We got in line for Thrasher's and sat on a bench facing the ocean to eat our fries. Two seagulls on the rail made Patsy wrap her arms protectively around our cardboard bucket, knowing the birds would steal, given half a chance.

"No way birds," she shouted. Her mouth was full of fries.

Patsy likes to steal things. Every time she says she *did a baddie*, I know she's stolen something of mine. A chocolate from my desk drawer. The ex-wedding band from my jewelry box. A book I'm reading. One of my red pens.

Our brother Fred lives in Ohio with his family, and last spring, when Dad was given his prognosis, six months to a year, there was no question of moving Patsy out there. For twenty-six years, her workshop has had a contract with the Baltimore Orioles, and Patsy loves the Orioles. She and her friends pack orange and black visors in boxes, glue pennants onto sticks, and tri-fold the season's calendars. She plays on a bowling team in Easton and eats brunch with friends on Saturdays. Patsy's best friend, Nora, another girl with Down's, died last year of pneumonia, but Nora's mother still has Patsy over to visit every Sunday. None of us wanted that to change.

When Dad had his first long bout in the hospital, he asked me to take Patsy. My house is only a few miles from his. Patsy keeps up the same lifestyle, more or less. Only she doesn't get to watch all the games with Dad, yelling, "O say can we see!" along with the TV, winding up for the first pitch. She no longer asks if she can see our father every day.

WE CHOOSE a spot on the beach for our two umbrellas, our blankets and bags. I rub sunblock over my sister's orchid-pale, soft skin. Patsy likes the green and white umbrella. I can sit for hours just watching the water, the foam rising closer to the towels, our little plot of land.

A family settles in beside us, drinking Cokes from a cooler and shoveling sand. The mother and father give their son a purple plastic scoop shaped like a heart. Patsy looks longingly at the Cokes. Nearby, the lifeguard in red shorts and a sweatshirt that says Beach Patrol drums her knees. Patsy peers over at the little boy.

In my bag is a stack of papers by ninth-graders, their first assignment of the year, on the discovery of Tutankhamen's tomb. I like teaching ancient Egypt, the pyramids and mummies. I tell them there are more than eighty pyramids, some you can visit, some lost in the sand. Ninth-graders like pharaohs and animal mummies, and we talk about monkeys, and falcons, and cats. We talk about the kids' pets, and what ties us to the past.

When Patsy moved in, she told me she wanted some new coloring books, so I shopped from an education supplies dealer and found *Alexander the Great: The golden relics of his life are illustrated here.* I bought her *Incas, Aztecs, and Mayas: The finest work of masterly Pre-Columbian artists,* and I bought *Civil War Heroines:*

Braver than a squad of generals, these daring women will inspire.
Patsy stays busy, even busier than me with my papers to grade.
She has never met a Crayola color she doesn't like. Alexander's
violet tunic flows over his mulberry horse. Incans in cornflower
masks dance among burnt sienna birds. Confederate flags wave
olive-green over maize fields.

She stares up at tanned girls who stroll past her blanket, arm in
arm, jewels winking in their bellybuttons.

"Patsy, you okay?" I ask.

"Not bad Cath," she says. "Not bad."

She rummages in her tote bag and pulls out scissors and a pad of
construction paper. I close my eyes. I can hear her scissoring down
the width. It's one cut every inch. Twenty-four strips per sheet of
blue, green, orange, red, yellow, black, and brown. She will put
these into various piles. The September wind blows cool over the
beach, and after a while, I open my eyes.

"Three black ones with the yellows, Patsy?"

"You know it Cath."

"Why the blues here, and this one green over here?"

She chuckles. "You know."

"I don't," I say.

Fifteen years ago, when our mother died, Dad told Patsy what
was going to happen, and she shut herself in her room for days. She
did the same thing last year, with the news about her best friend
Nora. Our father is eighty years old, and from the cancer, he is as
skinny as a mummy. Soon he'll be gone, and I have to tell Patsy
this fact.

"I have an idea," I say.

"What Cath?"

"Want to dig a hole?"

We kneel, intent on emptying a circular area of its sand. We dig with our hands. Patsy finds a clamshell and uses it to scoop the sand. We unbury things. A dime, some dry seaweed, a broken oyster shell. Patsy organizes these objects in a small pile.

The sun disappears behind clouds, and the family beside us packs up their plastic cooler. I bulldoze sand back from our hole. I reach my arm in up to the shoulder, and Patsy clutches sand in her fists. The little boy cries because he does not want to leave, and then they are gone. Patsy, who has been watching them walk away, suddenly laughs and flings sand at me.

"Don't, Patsy," I scold.

"What?"

I'm more irritated than I should be. I explain, "It's going in our hole."

"Uh-oh," Patsy says.

"And it might go in someone's eyes."

"Did a baddie."

"No big deal," I say.

My sister doesn't respond.

The cumulus clouds thicken. Our hole is deep enough that it is hard to pull out more sand without the edge collapsing. Patsy and I go stand on the ocean's edge and watch a small seabird hop up and down the surf. Out in the distance, the water looks like gray glass. Patsy goes back up to the umbrellas. I stay with the bird wetting his feet, racing into the retreating waves.

When I come back to our spot, Patsy is lying on the smooth

patch the family left behind. Her cheekbones glow with rosacea. She fiddles with her bag.

"Did a baddie," she repeats.

"What?" I ask.

"Sorry."

"It's just that we were trying to dig, Patsy."

Then I realize. Her *baddie* must be something other than tossing sand. But instead of asking for the truth, I blurt, "You know, Freddy's in town."

"My brother Freddy?"

"He flew in from Cincinnati."

She crawls over to me and rocks back onto her wide bottom.

"Today," she says, "Nora's mother is home alone."

"She is?"

Patsy nods, her legs crossed. My back aches. At the water, the gray and white sanderling advances and retreats. Pale head, straight black bill, he's looking for tiny crabs. The lifeguard talks in semaphore with another young kid down the beach.

I say, "You help out Nora's mother, right?"

And she says, "Nora always folded sheets. I fold the towels."

Patsy looks down. I can see the top of her flat head, her dry scalp, her funny cowlick. Her lips are chapped, and I fish in my pocket for lip balm. She bobs her head up and down unevenly, like ocean waves. Then she reaches across me into her tote bag to pull out a bright object. A purple sand scoop.

"I stole it Cath."

"Patsy," I say.

She asks, "What Cath?"

I point to the scoop. "Did you steal it, or find it?"

She stares at me.

I lean over quickly and rest my cheek on my sister's forehead. The wind blows in nice and cool. I think of her bundles of construction paper cut in strips. Why twenty-four oranges with six browns, Patsy? Why this bundle of all reds? The deeper sand in our hole is the color of sepia. I look down to where the birds dodge the waves. One sanderling cries to another, both running back and forth. It's a call like a high-pitched laugh, rising at the end. My sister holds the scoop by her ear and watches the ocean. Her face grays like the line between water and sky. I brush my eyes and see sea-green sand and magenta stars. My mouth is the ocean rushing in.

The Truth You Know

THIS IS THE APARTMENT BUILDING by Easton's railroad tracks where a lot of us live, like Zebulon Hoyle, Redge Preston, the blue-feathered girl. You already know it, the front's on Goldsborough Street, the eight double windows, one filled with empty cans of Pabst Blue Ribbon, one lit up with Christmas lights? Walk around to the parking lot, past this stoop, past Glenda's Wild Den of Tanning marked by hand on cardboard in the big bay. It used to be easier to find cheap rentals, but the western shore started bulging over the bay into these country towns. When the city people started to arrive, they gentrified the older buildings. What? Oh, about a year. Enough time to notice the brick crumbling at the corners and the wood chips missing from the stoop. People come and go from these dumpsters, where the blue-feathered girl plays on this strip of grass. A woman named Gillian Ash lived in my apartment before I moved in. They tell me I look a little like her. Go ahead, you can ask me your questions.

People live on every floor. I'll tell you about all of us, including Joan. I've seen her in moments she thinks no one's looking. She sneaks off with a Goodwill coat pulled over her combat boots to browse the art gallery or buy coffee at one of the new cafés. Joan Bishop is a woman wanting to be something she's not.

Yeah, our building is full of chumps.

Let's walk past this garage, up the flight of stairs. We will cross Zebulon Hoyle's apartment door, and the door to the apartment where Angela Gibbs used to live. Hoyle used to grin a lot, but since Angela Gibbs disappeared, he's only frowned. He thought she left him for a trucker, but I'm not sure he thinks that anymore. Last night, after his fifth of sixth beers, Hoyle came up to my apartment, begging for dirt on my next-door neighbor Redge.

That rusted Chrysler on the lot belongs to Hoyle. At night he's always tinkering. There's his cat, King, sitting on the hood. This chipped door goes to his apartment. Hoyle makes a living playing guitar down by the courthouse. If you see a slender black man, flat eyebrows over dark, grim eyes, singing at the gazebo by Easton's courthouse, that's Hoyle. He wears an old white derby. See how clean he keeps his windows? Unless he's been drinking, he sleeps only four hours a night, and he's loved only one woman his whole life. The white silk flowers in the window were meant for Angela Gibbs.

Redge, my next door neighbor, says Hoyle is a pussy. He apologizes to me for his language, but insists. That's why Hoyle's old wrecked Chrysler still doesn't run, he says. Hoyle isn't enough of a man to fix anything.

This door was Angela Gibbs's, this one here. Angela was ex-Air Force and beautiful like a goddess. She had long legs, hair like latticework, stiff little footprints in the black skin around her eyes.

Hoyle told me she flew a cargo plane in the Gulf War. I would come up the stairs and spy on her and Hoyle in his apartment, arms like a double helix, legs wrapped in a long batik robe. No one in this building closes the blinds. The slumlord's fixing up her apartment for the next tenant. Be careful, don't trip, the floorboards are uneven, and this ceiling is low. We're heading up to my landing now.

Hoyle can't manage his alcohol. Around seven o'clock last night, he knocked at my door and handed me a beer. He spoke about Gillian Ash, the woman who lived in my apartment. Her heart exploded. Hoyle said the girl with blue feathers noticed Gillian Ash's eyes swimming and called him, and Hoyle told me that Gillian Ash's mouth sucked and spewed and her heart burst through its walls.

Ash was a friend, Hoyle said, as if fighting something. Then he stumbled down to work on the engine in that Chrysler until it got too dark to see. I think a heart turning inside out gives him another dark thing to fear.

Someone came back late last night after Zebulon Hoyle had gone to bed. I didn't answer the knocking. From my bed, I followed the trail of headlights hung with fog. Something framed my vertebrae and braced my heart. I pounded my pillow into a nest. Shadows shifted like pages in the parking lot, but who was there? I dug into my pillow, hugging my breasts. When I woke up, there were new cracks above my window, and flakes of old paint had fallen like skin from the wall.

It might have been my neighbor Redge. That barking is his dog. Redge's door is always bolted, and people come up to bang and call out different names. They call him Pres, Reggie, Ray, Gee, Regis.

I call him Redge because he told me I should. If you ever meet a drug dealer with a tri-color dog, walk away. Redge has told me that Gillian Ash came and found him the day before she died, and he claims the dead woman bought a vial of crack.

Sometimes liars tell the truth.

Quick, there, look down on the lot. See the blue feathers quivering by the trunk of Hoyle's car? See her scampering away? That's the girl. She has a birthmark, a smudge winking just past her left eye. First time I saw her, I thought, that child knows more than she should. She smoothed past me like my own shadow, blue feathers pinned on the back of her head. Sometimes she plays a harmonica on my landing. No one knows her name.

I've heard from other people that Hoyle can unsettle steel with his guitar. The people from the cities, who mark their territory with flowers on streetlamps, stop and listen to him. They say his voice is rough and warm. When he throws his shoulders back, almost aglow, listeners become part of the music. Their feet tap, their pockets overflow. Children drop bills into Hoyle's white hat. He sings about how his parents died in the Cambridge riots. If you're listening closely, you might run.

Come on in. Sit at the kitchen table by my window. The sun is starting to set. Want a cigarette? We'll talk quietly because everything can be heard through these walls.

Before Redge Preston ever spoke to me, he strutted by this window sporting a handgun. One day, scratching his goatee, he said, Fleas on a dog's ass, girl, don't you think? And he said, My dog chews on stones.

That night, he invited me into his apartment, where we burned one, my weed on his ratty couch. He could tell I wasn't into him. Rubbing at a scar on his arm, he told me stories, some of which I'd already heard through the wall. The tales he tells expand in the heat like wood. His family is embedded down near Oxford. Sharecroppers, revolutionaries, slave owners, renegades. Great uncles deserting the Rebel Army, siring offspring, and deserting again. At first, I doubted everything, but he brought out evidence. Faded scrawl in a family Bible, a letter from a Cambridge hotel owner mentioning a fire and a cellar underground, a register from the Oxford Customs House tallying Barbados men. Redge let me smoke in his apartment while he spun worlds, and I was part of the wheel. I got the whiff of death. His stories don't have any morals.

Listen, it's pretty quiet now. Redge must be out. The dog's probably asleep. It's Redge who spread the rumor about Angela running off on Hoyle.

It was one month ago, right through this window, I saw Hoyle and Angela dancing in the parking lot. The whole building turned out to watch. The stars and moon were clouded over, but the headlamps of Hoyle's old car shone like spotlights. People from the front apartments crept out, and the feathered child capered like a monkey, both hands clasped over her mouth. Redge Preston slumped over the balcony, watching too. Hoyle's heels sparked up gold. Angela's braids and limbs drew our eyes like fire.

The next day Angela was gone.

Hoyle writes songs, Redge sells drugs, Angela lived off veteran's pay, and this is what I do every day. I wake up and shower, pull on a red uniform shirt and some khaki pants, and go down these back stairs. I buy a coffee at 7-11 and work at Safeway. I'm a part-time

checkout clerk. I checkout cartons of cigarettes. I checkout tomatoes and milk. I checkout chicken pieces, Kit-Kats, frozen pizza,
diapers, yogurt, pork rinds, Tylenol. It all progresses toward me
on the conveyor belt, slow as the clock. People ignore me, and I
sell them Tropicana and Coca-Cola and Absolut. When I'm tired,
I take a break. I smoke outside the entrance, watching customers
plod through the automatic doors, saying things in my head, like,
Go on about your business. I never speak, especially not to the reg-
ulars with their prune juice, K-Y Jelly, and ice cream. I don't want
to get involved.

Listen, that Joan Bishop who lives here is a rotten egg. She's the
kind of woman who wants to talk to everyone, who can ruin my
day. Close your eyes and imagine for a moment. Imagine a woman
living here tells you her father owns a corporation that manufac-
tures office supplies. Would you believe those lies?

I get my employee discount and buy my Camels and pizza. After
work, I like to walk by the blinking lights, the cans, Glenda's Wild
Den, other apartments with their closed eyes. I climb the scaffold-
ing past Hoyle's silk flowers, Angela's old apartment, Redge's mutt.
I water the plants on my windowsill. Then I sit at this table with
my smokes and watch. Redge leaves with his gun. The child wrig-
gles by, feathers flickering like blue flame. Hoyle mounts the steps,
ragged at the heart.

Hoyle told me that at first it was a steady pounding that Gillian Ash tried to pat into place. She hoped to keep it from her
lungs. The thing started to bang at her ribs like police at the
door. It grew louder, louder. Throbbed up in her throat, choked
down her stomach, thumped in and out all at once. Hoyle told

me that when it exploded, Ash's short fingernails went as white as window shades.

Redge says there's no one but Gillian Ash to blame. You don't smoke crack on a bad heart.

Joan Bishop's a chump. Remember what I said about office supplies? Suppose I tell you a figure that business might be worth. Say a woman doesn't want a house, or a husband. Does not want to host dinners, or improve the schools, or hang flowers on lamps. Doesn't want headaches. Suppose she surrounds herself with more serious troubles.

Truth rises, lighter than Hoyle's songs. Blanker than Redge's lies. When you try to hide something, it's like the bulging bypass or the façade of flowers or the fresh paint downtown.

How much is rent here? I pay two hundred a month, utilities included. Have another beer. Look, what would you do if you overheard something that you didn't want to hear?

Listen, the truth has to come out. Is it really almost seven-fifteen? I might lock the door. For a month now, my key has stuck every time I twist it in the lock. I have to press my body against the door to shut it, and then turn. I appreciate you being here. The night of Hoyle's last dance, the night Angela disappeared, I was sitting in this chair, smoking a cigarette, when she crept past in the cloudy gray light. It had started raining. I could see her on the balcony still in her flowing robe, knocking on Redge's door. She slipped in without a word. I listened through the wall. Angela's voice sounded like the rain.

I need it, she said. I need it, I need it.

Redge said, I'll make a delivery.

Angela said, You can't come down, he's not drunk enough.

Redge said, My mutt can smell liars.

He's not.

The dog snarled. Why stay with that faggot? Redge asked.

She said, Jesus, asshole, just give me my stuff.

A chair scraped the floor. There was a slap, a soft shriek, a gasp. A voice saying, Leave off. Barking. Then a thud against the wall. And suddenly, everything was quiet again. Redge appeared outside at the broken railing, dimly lit, touching his cheekbone. I watched Redge as he moved about the landing. The sky belched and vomited rain. Then I crept into bed and listened to the gutters clogged with water.

I hope it was Hoyle who came knocking last night. Yesterday evening he asked what I knew about Redge. What he's dealing, how much, who buys. He wants to put Redge away. Did I tell you how when Hoyle sings, listener and singer become one? Should I tell Hoyle about his girlfriend? The landing, and how Redge appeared with a limp batik robe? Should I tell him how the next time Redge and I spoke, he asked if I'd heard the news? And a deep scratch marked his cheek, and I asked, What news? And Redge sneered, Angela Gibbs climbed into a westbound rig at dawn.

Do you feel it? The table is shaking. Look out, stay in your seat. I thought it was simple, but it is not. Something inevitable is coming. It's Hoyle down there, back from work to ask if I'll help him catch Redge. You've heard about the woman who used to live in my apartment. How Redge sold her crack, and the next day she was dead. Is it hot in here? Joan Bishop's a chump, a waste of time, always chatting people up. Better to be quiet, watch the plaster chip away. We're all fleas on a dog's ass, someone else said.

The staircase is shuddering, or is that me? Hoyle is crying, Are you up there, Joan, Joan! Are you at home?

He will try my doorknob, gaze through the glass, and see you frozen in your chair.

It's not the ending I wanted.

I'm creaking at the knuckle. Hoyle's calling for someone who won't answer. My heart is hammering. My hand—Joan Bishop's hand—I admit it—sticks to the door. The harmonica sounds outside. Who dresses the girl in that button-down shirt, and where did she find the feathers, and is she six or twelve or older? Look, I'm lengthening my fingers around the wood panels and flattening against the pane. A weight presses on my foundation. My eyes are filling up with lights and signs. I don't know a way out. There is no other plane in the door. Run and tell someone a lie. Say you saw me smoke crack. Or tell the truth, that Joan Bishop was here, and that her hand turned into a handle, her spine twisted into a hinge. Say you saw the girl's blue feathers right outside the door, and Joan Bishop's heart vibrated at the frequency of the harmonica. The shafts of evening streamed into her eyes. Splinters spilled from her mouth. In just a moment there will be silence, but outside the apartment, the street will be paved with your feet. Go now, and tell this tale of where I have gone.

Lost Queens

I USED TO WORRY about my husband, Ben, because you never know what a person can take before he cracks. He wasn't easygoing before I died, but afterward, he tightened the screws. He pulled it together for the girls, married another woman for the girls. So then I worried about the girls who seemed like reruns of themselves, watching me with their big mouse eyes, me, lying on the bed with sunlight filtering through lace curtains like bones. The girls should be still floating around somewhere, lying on towels under a big beach umbrella, riding horses along trails, but they're not.

When I couldn't see them anymore, I worried about that. Ben had dressed them up for his wedding, Ashley in lavender and Haley, who just wanted her horse, in baby blue. Ashley soaked up the attention. I saw her swinging her long hair for the boys at Ben and Shelly's wedding. I would've cut her hair short. Neither Ben nor his new wife ever cut it short. A dear friend of mine was like that, couldn't put her foot down. Her daughter was my girls' babysitter, who got it in her head to compete for Miss Maryland Fire Prevention Queen. My friend asked me to come with her to see the contest, so I took Ashley and Haley to Ocean City to watch. Before the contest we jumped in waves and built castles in the sand. Then Ashley and Haley gawked at the babysitter in her pink gown. Ashley loved it. Haley, in her funny deep voice, said, "This makes me wanna puke." The babysitter lost. Oh, my girls.

I used to let the beauty queen know who was in charge. My friend appreciated it. Even after I died I would let that girl have it, like the day she drove up from a beach party to babysit. She was an hour late, and Ben and Shelly had left the girls alone to wait for her. When she walked through the door she was sucking on a peppermint. Haley felt my nudge and said, "Someone smells like beer." The beauty queen never made that mistake again.

When I got sick, Haley was only seven and Ashley was nine. That Christmas they lay around the house like two doped mice. I thought, "Buck up, little beasts, you're gonna face worse than this." I had already lost my voice. Ben was shaking like old wood, and I looked at him and hoped he wouldn't come undone. I prayed he'd remember what it was to be young.

Each day my friend visited me, from when they operated the first time until the end. At Christmas her daughter came to visit. I heard her out in the hall teasing Ashley and Haley, making them smile, bringing me back to high school when Ben and I fell in love and hiked mountains and smoked grass. I had told the beauty queen those stories.

There were no curtains over my bed. When the beauty queen entered the room, I could see the horror and the shut-off in her eyes. She had not imagined anyone could be a skeleton. She had a breakdown when I died.

The afterlife isn't what Ben and I imagined. It's like life. You wake up during the funeral and look around at the crying faces, all these people living in their heads, and you worry: Ben's controlling himself but not helping the girls. You worry: your own parents are coming to stay, old as they are, they cannot do this. You worry: Ben's asking his colleague from work to marry him, to take the girls to school, tote them to piano and riding lessons, guide their homework, tuck them into bed, and she's saying yes. It's like earth, but faster. You see: Ashley dresses up as a beauty queen. Haley falls off a horse. You see: Ashley loses her virginity. Haley pierces her tongue. You see: they get drunk together and vandalize the sign outside the fire department, *Queens Needed*. You see: Ashley writes heartbreaking poetry, Haley smokes pot behind Ben and Shelly's back. They try crystal meth together. You see: your daughters shooting up heroin, frantic and in control and free. You sit in the graveyard and watch and worry on your mound of earth, and then one morning suddenly, there they are, two fresh mounds on either side of yours. Ben's red hair is gray. How much can you take before you break?

The beauty queen has moved back to town. Sometimes she and my friend visit the cemetery. Her face looks like her mother's. This year I watched them hide Easter candy for the children. They tucked eggs into the flowers and grass on our mounds, and balanced rabbits on headstones, and poked chicks into divots. They hugged and even laughed, which is good for my friend, who often feels alone. The beauty queen also visits by herself. I can see her fretting before our graves, washing us with tears. Ben is all right. He loves Shelly and manages his life and cries less and less. The girls and I are not suffering. But the beauty queen? She's the one I worry about now. I want to put my foot down. "Take care of yourself," I wish to say, "and be content!" There is no other point. From the dead, this is what you need to know.

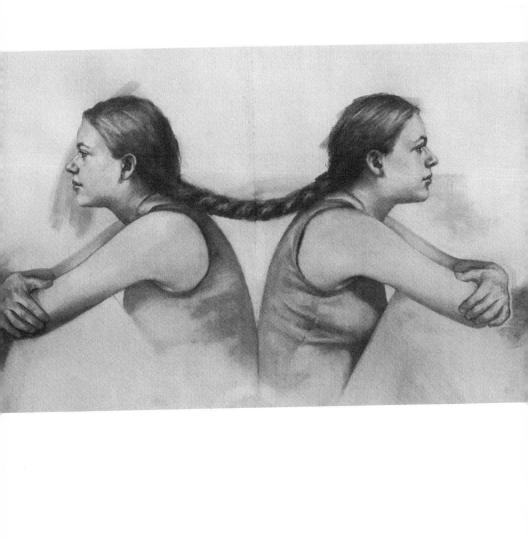

The Hole at Backyard Park

I. They Wished They Could Be Spies

INA SAID Father was actually a King, that's why their house was the castle, the biggest and prettiest house in Oxford, and Father had inherited a diamond ring, which he was hiding from the War. Ivan argued. Probably, he said, Father was a spy, in conference every night with the head spies, and that piece of jewelry was to be used for a bribe. Ina countered, saying that the War actually started due to Father discovering how to press diamonds out of sand, that Mother was helping cover up the truth—and Ivan suggested that Mother was a witch, half good, half bad.

On this thought they went wild: one day, Mother had gone bad, and she'd cursed Father, and that's why their parents had stopped talking to each other; Father, administering a truth-serum, had learned what she'd done; and Mother subdued him with a new spell every night, inflicting his awful tiredness, and giving him that strong, sweet smell.

And the skin around the twins' father's eyes folded down like his collars. And the secretive, musky smell kept on puffing out of his silver car into the carport and their Victory garden and their pretty house with dormers and painted trim.

Their mother acted as if their father's smell were normal. She never even yelled at him anymore. She was a lean, pale woman who painted a mole on one side of her mouth and carried herself nobly and volunteered at a Materials Collection Point in Easton. The twins often heard her tell people she was doing her part. Ivan and Ina decided that sometimes Mother turned invisible and only pretended to lock herself in her room. At night, she wandered the town like a shadow, sinking and rising over the Tred Avon River. Maybe Mother was not their mother at all, and all of this was her fault.

Their father, a terse, important man, worked for the Government, ferrying over the Chesapeake Bay to direct the manufacture of Warplanes all over the country. He'd commanded factories in Santa Monica, Long Beach, El Segundo, Tulsa, Chicago. The Allies would win with the aid of their father's planes.

As a rule, the twins spent weekdays ignoring their mother, running to kiss their father the instant his car pulled into the driveway on Friday night. The first time they smelled the cloying smell, they wrinkled their noses. They conferred before bed. Sticky, they said. Ina said it was like butter creams. Ivan said flowers, baby powder. Sometimes, working with Warplanes got you dirty, so this smell was engineers' special soap. Or maybe Father didn't get the smell from work. Maybe it came from a dessert he ate at a fancy restaurant.

This was around the end of Second Grade, or maybe beginning of Third, the twins could not remember, but for the rest of their childhood, they agreed that the smell came the year they were eight. And it stayed. By Fourth, the twins had almost grown accustomed to it. By then their parents barely spoke at the weekend dinners, only pass the potatoes, how's the meat, occasionally asking what Ina and Ivan had learned in school. "Nothing," they always answered. When pressed, the twins explained that they'd watched Sister Mary Pat trace cursive on the blackboard as she lectured the boys, who were less mature than the girls. After multiplication, their class moved on to fractions. They were into thirds, they said, one-third of six is two, two-thirds of six is four, three-thirds of six—

"Fine," Father said in the middle of their demonstrations. Their mother would dump more Victory garden potatoes on their plates, with her sternest eyes.

The War had ended then. After Fourth Grade, the twins saw their father more around the house. The smell went away, and their father did a little bit too. He seemed shrunken, somehow skinny, reading in his brown leather chair, or disappearing into his study. The twins still blamed their mother, but she also grew smaller and less clear. First her mole disappeared. Then her smile left. Then she seemed to fade into her naps, and the sternness left her eyes.

"Mother still loves Father," Ina announced one Saturday night when their father had taken their mother out to dinner. A babysitter sat on the parlor couch, a girl who'd brought a novel to read.

Ivan said, "He doesn't."

"You think you know more than me?"

"Go on, baby, think what you want. He doesn't love her."

That night, two of Ivan's fingers got bent backwards. Ina's lip got bloodied. The babysitter made them sit in separate rooms, and when their parents came home they were grounded for a month. It was cold outside, anyway, nowhere to go. Father said he would teach them games with cards.

They quickly learned simple card games, Go Fish and War. Mother looked on. She even smiled. No one had ever taught them to play cards? Then Father showed Ina how to hide a high card. Ina pulled out the missing Ace, and won the War. "No fair!" Ivan said.

"She can cheat if she wants to," Father told Ivan. "If you're mad, just quit. No one has to play."

The next weekend he showed them Gin Rummy. Then Poker. He showed Ina tricks, sleights of hand. He encouraged Ivan to walk away. Then, the last Friday evening of their punishment, Father returned to their house reeking again of that smell, the sick, burnt sugar smell, and there were no more games with cards. Ivan said it made him see pink. Ina said it was like Dracula's cologne. Their mother never mentioned it, the sweetness seeping out stronger than ever from their father's car, his suit, his pores.

When their mother left their father for a man who lived in Washington State, the twins were in Eighth Grade. They stayed in Oxford, living with their father through high school. Then, Ivan joined the Merchant Marines, and Ina went to college and got a degree and never married. She'd returned to be a teacher in Cambridge, and she lived with their father until his death, and then continued on in that same house, which was not after all a castle, in Oxford, Maryland.

II. But He Let Go

As IVAN flew toward Baltimore-Washington International, awake still in the last of his seventeen hours of travel from Macau, he thought about stars and how they looked smaller and smaller as

you traveled west. The narrow seat in which he held his body between rigid and slumped made him crabby, and when the steward-
ess came by with coffee he snapped at her, just like someone would
expect from an old expat. He wished he could turn things around,
make the plane reverse midair and head back to China, forget this
pointless trip. His stomach had almost done the job for him, two
days ago, heaving at the unfamiliar sound *You've reached Ina
Fellows* on his twin's answering machine. He'd had to stop from
throwing his hands over his ears at Ina's voice, which reminded
him of a crackling, expensive half-minute on the phone so many
years ago, the night he reached Bangkok, his first port city, when
he'd called home. Both times, a bad feeling had welled up inside
that made him wish never to speak to her, never to hear the sound
of her voice. But two days ago he'd left a message on her machine.
He didn't know why he'd said he was coming back, catching the
next available flight, but a promise was one thing he never broke.

The plane landed and he disembarked, picking up his own lug-
gage, traveling as lightly now as ever, and he handed Customs his
passport with shaking hands. The young woman in the glass box
looked at him once, twice, asked him was it true he hadn't been
back to the U. S. in fifty-eight years, and he nodded and said that
was about the truth. Then he marched over to a Hertz rep who
rented him a car and he got on the road. It wasn't so different,
being in Maryland, from any of the other countries where he'd
lived. Not until he reached the stretch of highway past Annapolis did he recognize anything, but for some reason, reaching the
Severn River Bridge reminded him that he hadn't been there thirty
years ago when his mother's second husband had died. In a letter,

Ina told him that she'd found Mother a nice retirement community right in Oxford, right on the Tred Avon River.

Once they'd dreamed the same dreams, he and Ina. After the divorce, their mother had made somber, yearly visits from Seattle, Washington, and during these visits she talked again and again of how she'd heard Ivan call, *Ina?* from his room, and his sister had answered from across the hall, *What, Double I?* Their mother had checked their beds and found them both fast asleep. It was wondrous! And Ivan had continued, *Ready for the mission?* and Ina responded with something that sounded like, *See you at headquarters.* The very last time their mother visited them before Ivan's departure for the Seamen's Institute, she'd brought two boxes of their favorite candies, soft sweet fruit and nuts covered with confectioners' sugar, and he and Ina had devoured a whole boxful, sitting on the sofa, as Mother told the story of their Headquarters conversation again. Had Mother hoped this dreamtalk meant something? A tender connection, perhaps eternal? Neither he nor Ina had shared much of their lives with Mother.

Mother had returned from the Pacific Northwest to die in Oxford. Crossing the Bay Bridge, Ivan thought about the fact that he hadn't returned fifteen years ago to witness their father mourning in Whitemarsh Cemetery. He'd read about it in another letter from Ina. Ina described their father leaning as heavy as ballast over Mother's grave. At the Kent Island Bridge, he started to picture what it would be like, meeting Ina at their childhood home. Ina's home. He and Ina were in their seventies now. What would it be like, walking through the front door and seeing her, an old woman now, his twin?

His head reeled as he drove down Route 50, taking in the sights.

A yellow Bob Evans and an Olive Garden had sprung up on the corner field of Chapel Road. The 1800s farmhouse with blue roofs had given up to a Holiday Inn Express. Ivan turned on Idlewild Avenue, passing a cluster of medical facilities, and found Oxford Road flanked by a new golf course. When he crossed the small bridge over Peach Blossom Creek, he thought of the night their mother had made the announcement, the summer before they entered sixth grade, that in September, the twins would attend separate schools. Ina would continue at Saints Peter and Paul, and Ivan would board at a military school. The very words of that night came back to Ivan. Their father had said *preposterous*, and their mother had said that Saints Peter and Paul's principal, Sister Genevieve, believed she'd *erred* in keeping them in the same classroom so long. Their father accused Mother of *going behind his back.* Mother said she guessed Father didn't have any *qualms about sneaking around*, so why should she? Father hotly said *go to hell.* The twins had said nothing. They'd been sent to their rooms.

That night in their dreams, he remembered, they had fought. They had yelled at each other and woken up crying in their sleep.

As Ivan drove over Trippe Creek, he felt what it might mean that he hadn't been back five years ago when their father, by then a very old man, had died. How everything had changed.

In sixth grade, he and Ina, on breaks and summer breaks, often talked about the kids they both knew from school, or from Oxford, kids who were still in Ina's class. By seventh, they avoided this kind of talk, as Ivan moved on to parade marching and playing lacrosse. The summer after eighth grade, when their father had brought them into his study, sat them down heavily across from his desk, their twin-ness felt uncomfortable and a little sour. Their father leaned on his elbows and informed them that their mother was leaving, as she'd *fallen in love with someone else.* Ivan clearly remembered how Ina had shrugged. *A no-one,* their father said, someone she'd volunteered with during the War. They'd looked away from his desk, toward the door. *Class IV-F,* their father continued, in a voice that sounded strange, *a weak heart.* Ivan had told his father that it would be okay. Ina had shaken her head. Their father had pulled him out of military school, and he and Ina had attended the same high school, but it was never the same.

Their mother's last visit before his own departure, when she'd brought the two boxes of candy, Ivan went out afterward to a high school basketball game. He returned drunk and found Ina eating the second box in bed. *Gimme one,* he'd said, and she did. *You believe it, us talking in our sleep?* he'd asked, leaning on Ina's doorframe because he needed it to keep standing. If he'd known these would be some of their last words for so many years, he might have—

Remember Headquarters? he'd asked.

Of course, she said.

What about the time we saw Father?

And Ina, damn her, the powdered sugar circling her mouth, said, *What time?*

That moment; her shoving Mother's candy toward him; his disconsolation; her defiance; sat in the pit of him. As he made his way down North Morris Street, trying to breathe calmly, he imagined sitting in the parlor sofa across from his twin, the parlor walls still painted lime green. He imagined relating travel adventures:

seafaring and ships, commerce and cargoes, women and foreign freights. He imagined her placid, adult years, and what he might have missed. On his face he wore lines of the ocean. On hers would be those of staying in one place. He would watch himself, try not to be rude or depressive, and perhaps Ina would bring up the old days . . . a hint of a sweet smell, a velvet box glimpsed in a desk drawer, a hole where they hid *as silent as stones*. . . . He swore to himself, coming within sight of Backyard Park, that he would not ask his sister what she thought of the knowledge of spies. He'd done well forgetting, letting the stories go.

III. Of What We Both Knew

THE YEAR WE WERE EIGHT, we were partners with equal interests, all votes unanimous. It was time to transcend the business of youth.

We terrorized other kids with lies. We seethed with scorn. We thought ourselves very like our father, agitated and important with the shape of work—gunners and turrets and ordnance—penned in his brow. Our mother would push her long finger to her lips, draw him into the living room with questions about Germans and Italians living in Baltimore and Annapolis, also the Japanese; the possibility of enemy agents; the probability of bombs falling over Washington. Using juice glasses against the wall to amplify their talk, we heard our mother say she'd been unable to sleep ever since the President had declared War.

Our house sat squarely on the street above Backyard Park. The second we broke free, we tore over to play and sling our fearsome tales. We dominated the slide, the swings, the maple tree, the merry-go-round. We issued warnings about the colony of sucking bats that had escaped from the Baltimore Zoo. Also the streak of tigers; the nest of pythons; the single, vicious vampire-cat, who might have snuck across on the Bellevue Ferry. We invented an infectious puking slobber disease, and the same day we told Faye Tucker that Ben Foster, her old crush, had said she was a *slimy sloth*, we convinced Billy Gardner, whose dog we coveted, to wipe his face with toad pee to repel monsters. It got so none of the kids would talk to us. That suited us fine.

The year we were eight, we had been temporarily separated without warning, midyear, by our elementary school. It was important, the nuns claimed, for us to learn to function apart. Our mother agreed and packed us off, ignoring stomachaches and missing uniform parts. Ina poured baby oil over a shelf of bathroom towels. Our mother picked her up and spanked her. After two weeks, Ivan started wetting his bed, greatly upsetting our father. Father took a day off from building Warplanes to insist that the Saints Peter and Paul nuns return us to the same class. At dinner that night, our mother's eyes were hard. She said the Sisters knew what was right for children, and Father should not interfere.

We kicked each other under the table. Father was our hero. Following his visit to Sister Marie's class, we took extra care to be good. We couldn't see why our mother looked at our father like that, her eyes like chunks of rock. When she said something about *important to nurture their individuality*, our father grimaced. When she added *over-dependent on each other*, he banged his fist. Our milk glasses spilled.

"What do you know?" he said. We lifted the tablecloth to cover our faces.

"I know a lot more than you can guess," she talked back. We ducked further under the table and could see her legs planted like two flagpoles.

"Sit down this minute," our father said. "Button your mouth."

At that, our mother's feet made as if to leave. Instead, she grabbed Ina's arm, who was sitting closest. "Children, up in your chairs." We sat back up. Our parents were looking at us, as if remembering something.

The year we were eight, and we'd been put back in class with each other, we slipped from our mother's grasp more and more. The first day of summer, she interrupted our whispering at breakfast. We looked at her, by the sink, wringing the dishtowel.

"Don't worry about us," we said. "We can take care of ourselves."

"You can, can you?" she said. "What about giving your mother a little help around here?"

"We'll be at the park." We ran from her lime and orchid rooms, the porch swing and lettuce garden. Carrying gear smuggled from our father's toolbox, a hand-held hoe and a trowel, we went to bully other kids away from Backyard Park. As soon as the coast was clear, we knelt by the merry-go-round. We loosened earth, pried out stones, and dumped dirt by the jungle gym and under the shrubs. Double Eye Headquarters was taking shape, in a hole that was soon deep enough for us to get inside.

"If we keep digging we'll reach the center of the earth," Ina said.

Ivan gloated, "Then Japan!"

We pilfered matches and an emergency blanket and stored them in the hole. There was a pile of pebbles, a battery-powered flashlight, a cigar box of marbles, and the leather collar off Billy Gardner's dog

Gunner. We stole gobstoppers from the Oxford Market for sustenance, and some of our mother's make-up to use for disguises. In Headquarters, lying on our bellies, we invented new tales, like the story of Gunner, a lost dog who was found by river trolls, who fed him, brushed him, gave him their favorite blanket for a bed, and let him live in their hole. Gunner loved the trolls. He saved them from dangers like earthquakes and floods.

By mid-June, we could sit up, legs crossed, in the Headquarters of Double Eye. We'd reached the block of concrete supporting the merry-go-round, and could hold onto the deep-set axle of the merry-go-round as the round wheel of it twirled over our heads. We were spies; we observed things from inside. We saw Faye Tucker, on the green bench under the maple tree, staring wistfully at one of the Flea Musketeers. We caught Sam Higginbottom talking to himself. We saw our neighbor, Mr. Whalley, picking his nose. When the Fleas started to poke around, we took the wimpiest, Ernie Brummell, over to the swings and told him that once a kid fell off the merry-go-round and was rushed to the hospital.

"They amputated both legs," we clarified. Ernie ran off to the other Fleas, dirtballs Olin Newton and David Wayne Bremer. "Faye Tucker has a crush on David Wayne," we yelled after him. When the Fleas came back as a gang, we were swinging high, arms crossed over the chains.

"There wasn't any kid whose legs got amputated," Olin said.

"Yes there was," Ina yelled. "His mother was a witch."

"She put a curse on the park," Ivan called.

"So if anyone falls off the merry-go-round, they automatically break their neck."

The Fleas trudged away. We observed them kicking the dirt piles around the jungle gym before they left the park. We scrambled into the hole under the merry-go-round. When Ernie, Olin, and David Wayne returned once more, they thought we were gone. The flat steel disk rotated above our heads. The axle creaked. Three pairs of shoes whirled by. When they tired of spinning, the Fleas dragged their feet to stop the merry-go-round, and they were extra cautious, and still Ernie fumbled getting off. We giggled. As soon as they were out of earshot, Ivan said, "We can perform real missions, soon as we dig to Japan."

"I'm sick of digging," Ina said.

"We can't stop now," Ivan argued.

The year we were eight, we overheard the story our mother told our father about how our voices had floated from our adjacent bedrooms down the hall, and she had gone to scold but stopped at one of our doors. We were not out of bed, she said to our father. We were mingling in our dreams, separated by bedroom walls. It was unusual, she said. It was very strange. "You see," she said, "the twins are upset as well."

Our father said she was overreacting. He said she was getting hysterical. He asked what we had said.

"Missions," our mother answered, "headquarters." She paused long enough to make us doubt what she said next. "And they mentioned you. And a woman in yellow, a spy."

"Yellow?" our father laughed.

"I know," our mother laughed back nervously. "It's the War."

Overhearing this story, we twins glanced at each other. Ina half-smiled. Ivan winked his eye. We were fail-safe allies. We could talk in our dreams and even read each other's minds. The year we were eight, all talk in our house turned into yelling. But we made out all right. We had a special gift, we could talk in our sleep. And a special destiny, which we often discussed: American heroes, Ivan and Ina, Double Eye Spies, champions of the War.

IV. If We Talked Now, What Would You Remember?
IVAN?

Yes.

Do you remember the terrible rainstorm in the beginning of third grade?

When Father wasn't home.

How Saturday during breakfast, the thunder punched our house, and the crashes bothered Mother, and she said for us to go play in our rooms, that she was going to lie down?

To soothe her head.

As soon as she disappeared, we crept back downstairs into Father's study?

We slipped in. You stood guard by the door.

And we heard Mother dialing the phone in the hall. I grabbed Mother's box of fruit jellies from the bureau. We could hear her whispering. I said we should run out into the rain. You suggested, instead, that we stay in Father's study.

It was dim in there.

From the storm. Outside the rain swept down. You explored, Ivan. You knelt and poked around the giant wooden desk, and used Father's flashlight to see in the drawers. I licked and stuck stamps. I drew entries in lined books and used a compass to etch circles. You found a bottle of Jack Daniels, sniffed inside, tasted it and coughed.

You were eating Mother's candies.

You flicked a pink and gray eraser at me that bounced off my knee onto the floor. The storm light flickered on strips of ticker tape and powdered sugar specks. I said, Bet there's a flood at Backyard Park. You were staring at something in one of the drawers. I said, Do you wonder what's happening down at Headquarters? Remember Gunner, that dog? And you did not reply.

You started listening at the grill of a heat duct. You said, If you're going to ignore me, then just come here and listen.

But then you hissed, Shut up and come look. Behind a three-hole punch, a container of pushpins, and a Dutch Masters box of cigars. It was at the back of a deep drawer. A black velvet box. You opened it and shone your flashlight on something glittering inside. A woman's heart-shaped diamond ring. We looked at each other. You said, Maybe it's a present for Mother. I said, Mother's on the telephone. She was always on the telephone, but she was crying on the phone. You came over with me to the grill covering the duct, and Mother was sobbing, and speaking through her sobs, the same words over and over.

I have had enough.

And we backed away from the wall and looked around at Father's study. The desk, the used stamps, the crumpled paper, the whiskey spittle. What a mess.

You said, No one has to know.

And we cleaned it up.

What did you mean? Know what?

Anything. We straightened the office and checked the hall. Mother was still on the phone, and we left through the back door, walked through the rain to Backyard Park. It was not flooded, but Headquarters, the hole under the merry-go-round, was filled with mud. We sat under the slide, shielded from the rain. I said, All they do is fight, and you said, We should run away.

And you said we should ignore them.

Rain streamed over your nose into your mouth. Father never yelled at us for using up the stamps or the circles in his books or the broken erasers. Mother never asked about her candies or why our clothes were filled with mud.

I went back and looked for that black velvet box.

You never told me.

It was gone.

V. Oh Brother, Come Home

Two CHILDREN hug the red rails of the merry-go-round at Backyard Park. After watching them for a moment, I walk over and plant myself on the bank of the lake. My likeness stares up from the water: spinster lips, thin gray hair, glasses that say hoot owl. The shrill metal platform sings on its axle, and my mouth in the water winces. These are not features my brother and I shared.

The two children move to the sandbox. Their mother wanly waits, sitting on my usual bench. The children do not dig toad holes. They dig as if their lives depend on it. Perhaps they dream of tunneling to the center of the world through to Japan. What does Ivan dream of now? I have waited so long to ask about his dreams and tell how, these days, I hear him crying in mine. Tell my brother how, in my nightstand, I hoard his cards mailed from port cities around the world, their postmarks mimicking the alphabet: Antwerp, Brindisi, Calcutta, Dunkirk; Taichung, Uddevalla, Vancouver, Wallaroo. On the first, which arrived long after his awful phone call, his note telling me that I should write to him, that we should stay in touch.

I want to tell him how, when I pull his postcards out from the drawer in my nightstand, I believe I read something like sorrow written between the lines.

The water wrinkles under the push of wind. Falling leaves alight, silver minnows dart and twinkle, and farther down, I see the hand-fed carp. Then the children are gone and the merry-go-round is abandoned. The woman, their mother, still sits on the bench. Why hasn't she gone with the children?

It is too quiet in the park.

A man, a blue and yellow stroller pushed before him, arrives. The woman smiles, and he kisses her on the lips, and she reaches into the carriage and lifts the infant into her arms. The young family heads toward the park exit. The father holds open the gate. She wasn't the other children's mother after all.

He's been absent from my life for fifty-eight years, my brother. Before he left, we created a rift never to be bridged. Maybe, maybe, we can cross it while he's here. If I can muster up the courage to remind him how, late that summer we were eight, we succeeded in driving everyone else away. Fewer and fewer kids came to our park, and those who came, left when they realized that we were there under the merry-go-round.

One afternoon there was no one but a woman who came and sat

under the maple on Faye Tucker's usual bench. Her mouth turned down as she waited for someone. We took note of her sundress, her dark sunglasses, her fake blonde hair.

"An enemy spy," I said.

My brother said, "Shh."

We were getting ready to toss a pebble, what we called the startle test, when over the hedge we saw the top of a man's head. Our father appeared at the gate, and because we'd never seen him near the park, it seemed impossible that it was really our father, but there was his car, parked nearby. He loosened his tie and looked around, and the stranger raised her hand and waved. Her sundress strap slipped down. We thought our father looked angry. He walked toward the bench. We put our fingers over our lips signaling each other to be silent like stones.

Our father went right over to the woman, who did not smile. For a while, neither he nor she spoke but just gazed around Backyard Park. They stared at the swings, then the slide. After about five minutes they started to talk, but we couldn't hear the words. Was it possible that our father was an enemy spy? Shifting to see more, my brother's head bumped the merry-go-round, and I muffled the clang. At the same moment, our father sat down and touched the yellow sundress. The stranger's hand pressed his arm, and then they clung to each other, she and our father, and they kissed and kissed. After a while our father stood. He and the woman left the park to drive away in his car.

When dusk fell we climbed out and raced to the slide, latched together, and descended fast. The maple tree blew in the wind, and the swings whined. We climbed the jungle gym. From the top, we could glimpse the other side of the Tred Avon. We discussed the habits of vampires and trolls; the possibility of stealing Gunner for our own; whether the President of our country dreamed about War. Our mother could be heard calling our names. We went back down in Headquarters, and stayed there a long time. We wondered whether if you love someone does that mean you have to marry them. Would we ever fall in love? Soon the flashlight batteries had gone dead. We crept out and gazed over the black water at the emerging stars. I asked my brother whether he believed toads could live in sand holes. He said, "I guess." He promised that someday, after the War, we would buy twin boats to sail around the world. I said, "We might." The sparkling sky spoke of a kind of loose eternity, spinning overhead close enough for us to touch, and many hours later, a lifetime of hours, we trudged up the street to our home.

Hold My Hand

THE RIVERS ARE WEIRD THINGS on the Eastern Shore, they're every-where, running like fingers from the Chesapeake west through rich people's properties to touch farmland, and never letting go. They're like veins in arms, or the knotty hands of watermen who catch the oysters that end up raw on gold rimmed plates at the Tidewater Inn. There's public access to all the rivers, parks and town docks and boat landings out on country roads, and they're mostly deserted at night, except for kids, boys and girls drinking and making out. That night, hanging onto the trunk of a big tree over my grandparents' old dock, while the police busted my brother and friends in the rundown cabin, I felt like the river was reaching out right for me.

You need to know, Richard Wooters, the ex-Boy Scout with scarred hands, told us, *there are two ways to do it. The Nazi Method uses fertilizer. Farmers lock up their fertilizer tanks so I use a method called Red-P. Iodine and cold medicine and matchbooks. Easy and way cool. Here's how you get the crystals. Take an empty Coke bottle and pour your iodine in it. Add half a bottle hydrogen peroxide and this much acid and chill.*

WE STARTED OUT SIMPLE, Josh and Brice and Dom and me. Josh, my big brother, had been my best friend since I was in sixth grade and he was in seventh, the year our mom died. Our father had always worked full-time at Agway, and back after Mom passed, my curly haired, big-nosed brother saved me from starvation. He taught me to toast bread and boil eggs for dinner. When I was in eighth grade, he talked me through a bad crush on Gabriel Brooks, a boy who would never like me back, and in tenth, he showed me how to drive a car, and smoke my first joint. My brother got depressed sometimes, it was a bad trait, but back when we were kids, he was full of zombie fights, bank heists, and plans to rule the world.

When we started brewing beer, Brice Hart and I were juniors at North Cambridge High. Josh had known Brice from Boy Scouts. They'd both quit, but my brother loved the Boy Scouts, the muzzle-loading, the archery, the survival kits. Like Josh, Brice Hart was a schemer. He was in Scouts for his dad, Dr. Hart, who said being an Eagle Scout would look good when Brice applied to college. Up until that year I had never liked Brice or his little brother, Dominick, with their pouty lips and bags under their eyes that made them look like rich kids, which they were, but that year in eleventh grade, when Brice and I were in the same English class, one day he raised his hand and said something about how *The Great Gatsby* was stupid because why try to become something you're not. It made more sense than what Mrs. Fellows, our old English teacher, had been saying, I smiled at him, and we sat next to each other after that. He started hanging out with Josh and me at Stewart Park, where Cambridge meets the Choptank River. His little brother Dom came along too, and one night at the park, Josh mentioned our grandparents' cabin on the Tuckahoe, a river that flows into the Choptank.

"You have a cabin?" Brice said. He cracked open a Budweiser and handed it to Josh.

"Grandpa left it to Dad last year." Josh turned to me. "Jenna, remember how Grandpa got high with us when we were watching The Fog?"

I was going to answer when Brice interrupted. "Does your father use it?"

Josh took off his baseball cap and rubbed his fingers through his curls. When we were kids, he and I got stranded once on the Tuckahoe. We'd taken Grandpa's canoe, and the tide had changed while we were out on the water. Our arms got tired of rowing, so we just floated farther and farther until Grandpa sent out a farmer with a motor boat to tow us home. Josh and I were always getting into trouble, and Grandpa was an old hippie, he thought it was funny enough to tell the story over and over again.

"He never goes there," my brother said. "Let's drive out! We can grab a .22, set up some cans."

"Sounds like a party," little Dom said. He was an eighth-grader then, a long-haired skinny kid.

I flicked my pull tab at my brother. It hit his chest. "How about a little Night of the Living Dead?" I said.

"Yeah, Jenna knows," Josh said. "It'll be our compound for when the zombies come."

Just a few feet away from us, the other side of the breaker rocks, was the Choptank. We sat there awhile longer on the Stewart Park picnic table, drinking beer, before we drove out to the cabin. The river hitting the rocks sounded like it was breathing.

Take a clean mason jar and put a filter on top. Pour the chilled stuff through. The black bits are iodine crystals. You'll need these for the cook. Now put your Sudafed in a jar with rubbing alcohol and then wipe off the sugar coating. Shake them in a bottle of Heet until they break down. Siphon off the top into a baking dish. Leave the bottom stuff alone or you will seriously mess things up. Fire up the electric hotplate. Cook until you get a white powder. Don't burn it or everything will turn out yellow. Scrape it off the bottom with a razor blade. Don't breathe it in because this shit will give you a headache like you can't believe.

FROM CAMBRIDGE the cabin was about ten miles northwest. You crossed the Choptank toward Easton, cut north, hit a small paved road, and then turned down a dirt lane surrounded by woods. That first night, we parked Brice Hart's Land Rover by the back stairs leading down to the dock. The canoe lay on its side. We walked uphill and through the kitchen and the living room and ended in the basement with its sliding doors looking out on the woods. My brother and I flopped on a couch. Little Dom looked at the bookshelf. In the storage closet, Brice found some enormous glass containers and a refrigerator holding dark bottles.

"Hey, look at this," he called.

"That's beer Grampa made," Josh called.

We toted some down to the dock, it tasted like bitter caramel, and that's when Brice hatched the plan to start selling beer to the kids at school. Boom, easy cash. His beer scheme never would have worked if it had been up to him, but we all got pumped about it, especially Josh, he found a book filled with recipes Grandpa had underlined. "Zymurgy," Josh read, "now there's a million dollar word."

A waterman who ran a homebrew supply store on Kent Island helped us choose malt grains, hops, yeast, and priming sugar. Our first batch was like a magic trick, steam and smells making us laugh. It fermented for two weeks and sat bottled for two more, and when it was ready, all sixty bottles, we partied until we passed out on the dock. I still remember the glitter of sun the next morning and the colors on the Tuckahoe's brown face. The river had its blue eyes, and gold off the sky, and green from trees. Brice had gotten up first and he came stomping down the wooden stairs. "We're going to be rich," he said.

"Dude," my brother yawned. "You're already rich."

If we were going to make it, Brice continued, we needed more stuff, a crystal thermometer, glass carboys, rubber tubing, and we could brew three batches a weekend, he figured, twenty-five six-packs, around three hundred dollars profit a week. My brother was a senior and wondering what he was going to do after he graduated, so he liked the idea of money, and of course so did Dom and I.

That spring when I was a junior, we hung out at the cabin a lot. Most weekends, we sold beer to kids who partied, loads of them at North Cambridge and Easton High. My brother graduated with plenty of cash, and that was a great summer, swimming in the Tuckahoe, and taking the canoe out past muddy banks to explore side streams swimming with fish that never got caught.

There were some catfish that looked the size of my arm. In August, Josh enrolled in a few classes at Chesapeake Community College, and the four of us still brewed every weekend. I spent my money on a hi-fi system and told Dad, who didn't care much anyway, that I'd gotten the money babysitting. One night after we had finished boiling malt and hops for an ale, we stuck the enamel pot in a cold bath and sat on the dock to wait. I remember dipping my hand in the water, and at night, you couldn't see the Tuckahoe but you could hear plenty. Owls hooted, crickets squeaked, and sometimes a turtle or giant fish splashed. Downstream, lights twinkled in the trees, security lights on some river estate. I was getting low grades in most of my classes, but I hadn't started to worry about what I'd do the next year because life was fine, and the water, when I touched it, touched back.

In the moonlight, Josh took off his red baseball cap and rubbed his head. He looked skinny. I hadn't been seeing him during the week because after school I pretty much locked myself in my room with my music, and he never showed up for dinner. "So Jenna," he said, "there's this kid Brice and I know who used to be a Boy Scout down in Wicomico. He's figured out a way to make real money."

Over the Tuckahoe, bats flitted, they caught insects, and the lights downriver blinked like snake eyes.

"His name's Richard," Josh said. "He makes a couple thousand a week. If we start out small, just a couple grams—"

"Grams of what?" I said.

"Crystal meth," he said. "You cook it out of household stuff, just the boxes of Sudafed that we have in the bathroom would make two or three grams. The stuff turns to gold." He put his hat back on, which hid his face from me, and I watched some clouds shade the moon and the river. Brice and Dom were quiet, unusual for them. Later that night up in the cabin, while we were playing poker, I found out I was the last one to hear my brother's plan. Brice had already done the math, knew that a gram sold for a hundred-fifty dollars. Little Dom, still in Scouts, knew kids who knew Richard Wooters and had talked to them about the whole thing.

"But if anyone buys a lot of pseudoephedrine, the store notifies security, right?" Brice said, and I looked at him slit-eyed because he'd just bet all his chips, and I had a pretty good hand.

"So this week we go shopping in Cambridge," my brother shrugged, "and somewhere else if our first cook turns out."

I laid down my full house, Brice showed four aces, and he said to me, "You'll pick up the iodine?"

"Damn it," I said to his cards.

"They sell it for horses. You're a girl," he said. "Girls love horses."

Little Dom snickered. Maybe he knew about the time Brice took me to Dover Downs to bet on races and tried to kiss me.

I hated not knowing this Boy Scout buddy of theirs, who apparently had scars from mess-ups and fires in his cooks. When Brice mentioned the scars, little Dom said, "But he makes, like, a *ton* at a time." My brother started telling about a white trash guy he knew at Chesapeake College who'd gotten addicted to meth, his arms wasted with sores. Stupid, Josh said, you can't let yourself get addicted, and I should have heard something in my brother's voice, but Brice was already calling the ex-Scout's cell phone, and next thing I knew, we were planning our first batch.

Our shopping trip was fun, we parked at the movie theater and entered Wal-Mart one at a time, like in some movie. Josh bought drain opener, aluminum foil tape and acetone. Dom got a digital scale. I picked up a packet of Contac twelve-hours, and Brice, a box of Sudafed that he had to sign for. Then we went to CVS for the iodine tincture, no one questioned me, and Josh and Brice got Coleman Fuel and razor blades from their house. I grabbed a hotplate and some boxes of old mason jars Mom had packed away in the attic.

Richard Wooters, long-haired and nerdy looking, wore a faded Grateful Dead t-shirt. He admired the cabin and the river, leaned toward me, and said you had to have a gentle touch to be a good cook. When I rolled my eyes he backed off. He poured our chilled mixture over a coffee filter. Brice wrung out the bundle to get our little black iodine crystals, I counted pills, Dom worked on the phosphorous, and Josh evaporated liquids. What was left over reeked like a mix of camp fuel and garlic. Richard Wooters suggested that we bury it in the woods. Josh said no, we should drive it in to a town dumpster. Brice said that was asking to get caught. In the end, we poured it in empty Coke bottles and stuck them in the closet. Richard bought our first efforts for two hundred dollars, and the second, and the third, and so on, and later, when we were producing too much waste to store, and the winter ice thawed, we dumped all the bottles downriver.

That winter, Josh started looking kind of bad, it reminded me of the summer vacation after Mom died, when my brother got so sick he fainted on the playground. We were playing foursquare, and he'd jumped after the red ball and kind of tripped and passed out, knocking off the baseball cap he'd always worn. The other kids ran up our street and got our father, and as I sat with Josh, who'd bitten through his lip and bled all over his yellow shirt, I'd gotten so scared that I passed out, too. That was the summer after sixth grade.

My sixth grade was a year of primary colors, starting with the afternoon my homeroom teacher handed me the blue and red and yellow school envelope that contained a letter to my parents about my standardized test scores, best in my class. The yellow school bus dropped me off at home, where our Grampa in his frayed blue fishing pants stood at the screen door and asked, "Jenna, sweetie, how you doing?"

I remember saying I was hungry.

"I'm going to give you a ride over to the hospital. Your Dad's waiting for you there, with Josh. Your Momma's getting checked over."

Grampa piled me into his red truck, hospital hallways swirled yellow, and then it was blue, my dad leaning over a bed, and Mom wrapped in a blue sheet. Dad straightened when I came in the room, and Josh was nowhere to be seen. "She's dead," my father said. His eyes were dry and flat. All I could think about for a long time was the striped envelope I never gave to anyone, and yellow hospital walls, and Dad's blue eyes, and Grampa's truck. That summer vacation, when Josh passed out on the playground and his hat went flying, the world went black for a long time. I woke up to him over my face saying, "Jenna! Just cause I pass out doesn't mean you do, too!" It turned out Josh hadn't been eating for a while. The doctor gave our father orders to go grocery shopping. Dad shopped and worked, Josh started cooking for me, I made sure he was eating, and slowly, the colors returned.

*This is how to get the red phosphorus. Fill a coffee cup with ace-
tone. Take boxes of matches and dip the strike pads. Scrape off the
phosphorus with a razor blade and let it dry.*

ONCE, as we counted our profits, my brother said that the four of
us were like a good hand. "The hand is quicker than the eye, Jenna," he said to me, like it was some magic secret. We made a good
hand, and that was why we'd never get caught. Who's the thumb, I
asked. Josh said that was Richard Wooters, because he sold everything we made. It wasn't until the next year, after I graduated high
school, before I had to make any real decisions about what I was
going to do with my life, that Richard Wooters told us to start selling for ourselves. He gave Josh a list of addresses where we could
make deliveries. The first place was a mess, a trailer home in a field
outside Easton, just off Kitty's Corner Road, with a blue swing-set
rusting in tall weeds and piles of burned trash dotting the yard.

Dom and I stayed in the car, windows rolled down, while Josh
and Brice met our customer, a man in skinny jeans. He walked as
if someone had duct-taped his hips. "Hey, kid, you got ice?"

When he said that, we saw his front teeth were missing. Dom
thought everything was hilarious, and he and I laughed in the car,
faking coughs into our hands.

Brice stood on the edge of the road. "Sure, man. You have our
money?"

The man waved toward the trailer. Dirty blinds hung in the
trailer's windows, and a blond woman slouched out from the door,
her skin gutted with sores. "She got it."

Josh handed the man a bag. I was looking at one window, tiny fingers poked through the blinds, and I couldn't see a face. I nudged Dom, but the little hand had disappeared.

The customer hacked and spit. "You college boys?"

"Chesapeake," Josh said.

"This crank looks cloudy."

"No, try it," my brother said. "It's good."

"Ritchie Wooters says you okay, but I believe it when I see it," the guy drawled. "Guess what, college boy, I don't see it."

I was still staring at the trailer to see if whoever belonged to that hand would peek out when the man's fist connected with Brice's stomach. A second punch pounded into my brother's jaw.

Josh's head hit the asphalt, and Dom and I jumped out of the car.

From the guy's back pocket came a switchblade. "Don't let Penny out the house," he yelled at the chalky woman who now seemed made of string, stretching in every direction. "Who now, ladies? Who wants a taste of me?"

Dom grabbed his big brother and lifted him toward the car, I helped my brother to stand, holding his face, looking at the bloody spot on the asphalt where his mouth had been. He spat out a chip of tooth. I got him into the car, my brain flashing from the little hand in the blinds to us.

You got to measure materials and prepare your cookjars. Weigh your pill powder and an equal amount of crystals. Divide the weight of your powder and crystals by three and that's your phosphorus. Poke holes in the lids of two jars. Insert a tube. Fill one jar halfway with distilled water. Lid it and seal. Now put your iodine crystals and pill powder in a jar and add a little distilled water. Set it on the hotplate and add the phosphorus. You'll get an immediate reaction. Get the lid with the hose. Screw it on tight. Turn your hotplate up high.

I REMEMBER LIKE IT WAS YESTERDAY the night we met Alex Johnson at the Canvasback Pub. It was a Thursday, we'd all gotten in with our fake IDs, even though the bartender knew who we were. Brice was drinking whisky, talking to a couple girls, and Josh and Dom were tossing darts. A band I liked, Blue Miracle, was playing, and I stood at the foot of the stage, not noticing the guy to my left until the song ended. I bumped into his arm, spattered his cup of beer on the floor. He looked a little older than me, maybe two or three years. Everyone around us clapped and whistled. He wiped his wet sleeve on his jeans.

"Sorry," I said.

He smiled and held out his hand. "No problem," he said. "My name's Alex."

"I'm Jenna," I said. He looked familiar, but I didn't know him. "Are you from out of town?"

"No, I live here."

"Oh," I said, trying to remember where I had seen him before, maybe he was older than he looked.

"I needed out of Baltimore a couple months ago," he said, "so I moved down here. Got a job at the pawnshop on Route 50."

"What were you doing in Baltimore?"

"Failing out of Towson State. My third year wasn't going so well."

Over his shoulder I could see my brother looking at me. I should've said goodbye to this stranger, I should've known better, but he seemed okay, not a stuck-up-home-from-college guy, and not a total redneck, and not someone I'd known forever, maybe someone who could see me for what I wanted to be, even though I didn't actually know what that was. I brought Alex over to the bar and bought him a replacement beer. The rest of the night, we talked between sets. Brice joined for a while and cracked a stupid joke about buying me a sex-on-the-beach, and I told him to go find someone who liked that drink. Standing a couple people away, my brother twirled his baseball cap and scratched his head. Finally my new friend said he had to be at work early the next morning, he looked me in the eyes and smiled, and then he left.

Brice came over and poked my side. He said, "I got a feeling about that guy."

"What?" I said.

"He looked at you the whole time."

Little Dom was listening. "Something wrong with that?" he asked.

My brother came over. "Who was your friend?"

"His name's Alex Johnson," I said.

Josh nodded. "I've seen him around."

He walked me back to our house that night, rather than staying out later like he often did. At home, Dad was passed out on the couch with the television running. Josh said he'd been wanting to tell me something and he followed me to the door of my room.

"What," I said.

"I've tried it," he said. "Once in a while. And I really want to do it with you, Jenna," he said. "Just one time, and then neither of us will ever do it again."

I had never turned down one of Josh's crazy plans. He made me promise not to tell anyone, and that night, we turned up my music and snorted crystal through a straw, and after half an hour, I felt happier than I had in months, despite the fact that the summer was almost over and Josh would start classes again, and Dad had said he was going to charge rent if I didn't make up my mind what I was going to do. Soon I'd have to decide, find some actual work, or go to Chesapeake, which sounded worse than a job waitressing or working retail.

"How many times have you done this?" I asked my brother.

"A handful."

We both danced for a while, and laughed, and then we just talked, making plans, how we'd move west, maybe to California, I'd get a job at a record store, and Josh could start importing stuff from Mexico, or maybe finish school and become a lawyer or something. We had to save up money, Josh said, and he got a funny look on his face. That guy I'd been talking to at the bar, he said, might be into meth. Ever since the knife incident we had only sold to people we knew, and we checked out new people before we would sell. I didn't want to say I hoped he was just into me. I said he seemed clean. My brother looked at me, and his face was sad. Just before I fell asleep, he was about to go out the bedroom door.

"Do you remember that time I hit my head on purpose at recess?"

"On purpose?" I said.

"It was stupid," he said. "I never told you."

"Why?" I asked, but he had already closed the door.

In the morning, I woke up feeling fine, no hangover. I went to the kitchen and made coffee for Josh. Our father was up and gone. I walked down the hall to my brother's room, poked him in the chest, and he grunted but didn't open his eyes.

"Hey," I said, bending over his bed. "We gotta go make some money."

Josh reached up to his bedpost, eyes still closed, grabbed the red baseball cap, and shoved it onto his head.

The cook's done when the contents stop boiling and everything's gooey and black. The black shit that smells like rotten egg is your dope. Add some distilled water and run it through a filter to get liquid the color of honey. Add some Coleman fuel and Red Devil Lye. Shake it. Siphon it into an empty bottle. Avoid the stuff on the bottom of the jar. Add a little more distilled water and one drop of muriatic acid. Put the cap on and shake the hell out of it and set it somewhere upside-down.

THE NEXT WEEKEND at a lame party thrown by a rich kid, we ran into Alex Johnson again, who invited us back to his place, an apartment over the jewelry shop downtown, and when we got back there Brice pulled out a joint and passed it around, and my brother said no thanks, he had plans later. As little Dom and I smoked the joint, I started to see that Josh's sixth sense was right. Alex told us he knew people looking to score some meth, he asked me to walk him down to the corner store to buy a soda, and on the way, separate from the others, I said I might be able to hook him up. He shook his head, and that's when I learned that Josh had already sold Alex two grams. I gave him my cell number anyway and threw in directions to the cabin in case he ever wanted to visit.

I didn't tell my brother about my thing for Alex, and there wasn't much to tell, just that he left me text messages, simple things—LTS

GT 2GTHR—WR RU—that got harder to figure out—WAYD—YY4U—and I would always write back for more. But then he quit the pawn shop, he was on the road a lot, never had time when we could get together. Still, we texted enough that I kept up my hopes.

After making a couple of mid-sized purchases for his friend in Baltimore, Alex disappeared for a while. When he phoned me one day, after I hadn't talked to him for several weeks, he asked if we could all meet up at Stewart Landing, not just me but Dom and Brice and Josh, too. I was disappointed but I called Josh, who got hold of Dom. At Stewart Landing, I could tell that Josh was high on meth. He heaved rocks from the breaker wall into the Choptank, stomped back and forth to the cooler, and couldn't sit still. Alex arrived in a beat up brown van, and I asked where he'd been, what he'd been up to.

"There was an accident in Crofton." Alex's voice was quiet. "A friend of mine, Katie, she got hurt."

He'd never mentioned someone named Katie before. My stomach sank.

Brice asked, "What kind of accident?"

"Explosion in a meth lab."

"You were there?" I asked.

"Just heard about it," he told me with a long look. "I was up in Philly." Then, just like that, he asked if we'd sell him thirty grams, a larger batch than we'd ever made. After a couple moments of calculation, Brice announced that we could probably have it ready in two weeks.

Josh threw a bottle of beer to Alex, who caught it in one hand, and I saw my brother thinking something that he wasn't going to say. "Dangerous, got to be careful," he said instead. Alex opened the bottle of beer, and it sprayed in every direction. Josh laughed, jumped onto the picnic table, licked his lips, and took off his red cap. "Got to be careful," my brother repeated. He scratched his head. "You heard of Siegfried and Roy? Guys had it down to a science, then *boom*, tiger attack. There's a market, Brice, if magicians did meth, we'd have some seriously fast magic, fast cash, fast like they can't say no—"

"Man," Brice said, "chill."

My brother bounced on his toes, he put back on his baseball cap and jumped down, too quiet, and I thought about giving him a hug, holding him to the ground like a helium balloon. No one said anything.

Alex stood up then. "Got to go, guys," he said. "See you in two weeks. Jenna, wanna go hang out at the Pub?"

I gave a thumbs-up, glanced at Josh who wasn't looking at me, climbed into Alex's dirty brown van, and we were gone. After we turned a corner Alex suddenly remembered he had somewhere he had to be, and he dropped me off at my house. He didn't call me like he said he would, and the next night, and most nights after that, I was busy cooking for the big deal.

It was like in the movies, a crystal chandelier over our heads, the chain about to break, and we had no idea. Josh scratched bright red lines on his arms. Brice shook a mason jar, eyebrows arched, jowls like his father's. Dom's eyes glittered. On the last batch, the night before our delivery to Alex, I threw down a piece of coiled tubing. I said, "We can't keep doing this."

My brother grabbed my elbow, his pupils like black pools.

"Jenna, here in the old cabin, Night of the Living Dead, man. We're all in it together."

It didn't seem like Brice and Dom got that Josh was high.

"You know," I said, scraping powder into plastic baggies, frustrated with all of them, especially my brother, but I couldn't find more to say. My phone vibrated in my pocket. *PUB 2NITE*, it said. I slid open the glass door leading down to the river. I punched in, *OK*. I said, "I'm taking a break."

I thought I'd hitchhike into Cambridge, but instead of going up to the road, I walked downhill through the woods, smelling leaves and dirt. On the dock I dangled my legs over the surface, the Tuckahoe smooth like glass, and I stayed looking at the river for a while. Then I climbed back up and watched my brother and my friends through the sliding glass doors. They were framed in the cabin lights, Brice draining water from a bottle, Dom staring into a bowl, and Josh, skinny, shaking. His forehead glistened with sweat, the color of sickness.

When the cars pulled up at the front of the cabin, the engines switched off, and someone banged at the cabin door. I felt so afraid.

"Police," a voice yelled.

Brice knocked little Dom aside and ran up the stairs to the front of the house. Little Dom opened the sliding doors and ran out back, near to where I hid, but he turned up toward the road. Josh started stuffing crystal into his mouth. Eyes wild, my brother gulped, peered through the opening into the night. Did he know I was watching? Did he hope I'd get away?

I held my breath against a tree on the edge of the ravine. Four cops stormed the cabin and handcuffed my brother, who lay limp on the ground. They caught Dom, too, and he hunched, cuffed, ten feet away from me. Brice had bolted. And Alex, Alex Johnson, a fucking cop, got illuminated by the fluorescent light gleaming out the cabin doors and the moon shining its full glow.

He took his time photographing two-liters filled with black gunk, dirty coffee filters, gallon jugs and mason jars, rubbing alcohol, and punched-out pill sheets, bright flashes making shadows on all the trees. For a moment, he hung the camera on his holster and sniffed at a jar. I leaned into the thick old oak tree and could really see, then, the wide shoulders over his narrow waist, the shaggy blond hair that hung over the lines around his eyes. He was not part of a good hand, and we all should've known better, especially me. Alex rounded the corner of the cabin, it had been about fifteen minutes since I'd seen my brother swallow so much of the cook, and in that moment I hated them all. Alex, Brice, Dom, even my brother, who looked like a zombie, his skin glowing white, his blue hat covered in dead leaves. I had a sudden picture of Dad sitting at the kitchen table reading the paper, ready to leave for work, eating a bag of pretzels. I stuck out a foot to run but instead, I kept hugging that tree, the river flowing behind me.

Almost done. Get the hotplate up to 400 and set a bowl on top. Take your bottle upside-down with separated fuel and water and loosen the cap. Drain the water into the hot bowl. You want it to evaporate. Take a coffee cup and add this much acetone. Once the water in the bowl has disappeared put on your yellow gloves. Take the bowl off the heat and add another splash of acetone. Swirl it

*around. Don't let it touch your skin. Don't breathe in. If you did
it right you'll see crystals on the bottom of the bowl.*

THE OAK TREE pressed hard on my shoulder. Uphill were cop cars
and dirt road, and downhill, the Tuckahoe. If the river could feel,
this is what it felt like when we dumped our waste in it. Dom was
muttering, "Piece of shit, piece of shit." He didn't know what my
brother had done, neither did the cops, and I wished Josh would
moan or scream or roll so I'd know he wasn't dead. A branch
creaked over my head as if it wanted to talk, and in the near dark,
Alex, the narc, walked over to Josh and Dom with another cop
whose gut pressed against his shirt buttons. Flashlight beams swept
over the scene. Blood ran from Dom's nose onto his face and shirt,
and he was crying, and he spat on the ground.

"Doesn't stink much," the fat cop said. "What'd they do with
all the waste, Bob?"

"I was never around for the cook," Alex answered.

The two turned to Josh, a lump on the ground. The fat cop let
out a *hrrr* like a cow and said, "What about that one?" My heart
thudded. At the side of the cabin, another flashlight appeared. It
halted ten feet away.

"Buckley caught Brice Hart out on the road," the other light
called.

"That's it then," Alex said.

"Better get them in," said the fat cop. "This one on the ground
doesn't look too good."

The third light walked over and looked Dom up and down. "Dr.
Hart's not going to be happy," he said. "Where's your girlfriend, kid?"

"Oh, Jenna Williams," Alex said loudly then, like he was calling me, and I almost answered. "She wasn't as involved as I thought. Looks like she wasn't here tonight."

Dom stared at him. My head roared. If I'd told Josh and the guys about my crush on Alex, or if I'd wondered more why Alex and I never moved beyond cell phones, maybe I'd have predicted *Bob*. Did Dom imagine I'd known about this bust?

"Let's get moving," said the fat cop.

"Let's take this one up," said the other one, "and then the druggie."

They led Dom up the hill and left my brother cold on the ground. I was shivering behind the tree, nothing clear in my head. I pressed my forehead into the rough bark until I was sure there would be blood. In a heap on the ground, his moonlit face up and his hair streaming back, my brother looked so little. Get up, I thought. Voices yelled at the top of the hill beyond the house. Brice was probably trying to outtalk the police while Dom fought not to get in the car. Then Josh cried out, his voice weak like he was in pain. I ran to him.

He twitched and gagged. His skin was hot and deadly white, and his eyes had rolled into the sockets. When I pushed him onto his side and cradled his head, vomit spread through my fingers. Two voices came down the hill. I heard the word *ambulance*.

"Josh, Josh," I whispered. In a moment, they'd arrive. "Josh," I said, "I'm still here." Josh's cheekbones glowed like in the movies where it's nighttime but you can see everyone's faces. His eyes were closed. I wiped the vomit from his mouth, and a breeze blew up at us from the Tuckahoe. I looked down and behind me at the river, and I stumbled backwards down to the dock, and pinned myself against the rough wood. The cops would come back, they would heave Josh up into their arms, their sirens would wail away through the woods, echo over the farms, and cross the bridge over the Choptank, calling until I couldn't tell what direction they called from anymore. I put my fingers in the river, took them back out, put them back in. Brice and Dom's parents would post bail and hire lawyers. I imagined our father at the kitchen table, what he'd say if the police called, and how Josh and I had saved up a thousand bucks. I knew that if I hitchhiked up to Cambridge, grabbed our cash and boarded a bus, I might leave the Eastern Shore, but I could never disappear. Downstream, lights blinked blindly. The water held the edge of the dock, the moon in the sky, the trees leaning into it, and my hand.

Flesh Ring

Old Woman Sleeping

IN MY DAUGHTER'S HOUSE it snows. There is the bureau where I set my trunk. There is the table lamp. There is the poinsettia on the windowsill. The poinsettia is red and green but at night it's black and gray. There is the book of awful photographs Teresa showed me this afternoon. Why did she show me that book?

My daughter worries about her son. Gabriel cannot be the scoundrel they say he is. I blame my daughter for raising him the way she did. I said it when her father bought the big river house and again when I left the Eastern Shore. I had to get away from that small town life. Now I'm back to die. Gabriel has torn up his roots and gone off to a West Coast city to huddle on the street. Teresa says he is like his Uncle William, always running. I say he is heartsick over some girl.

See the lamp lighting up snow. There is the open closet. There is the mirror where this afternoon my daughter stared at her face. She came in with medicine and planted the tray on the chair. She brought her camera and took pictures of me on this bed. Who snaps pictures of her mother's death? In the mirror she pinched her cheeks. Her husband Harry has gone prematurely gray. The tray she planted on the chair sprouts roots. There is no earth, only pavement.

My grandson Gabriel holds up a sign. It is too far away for me to read. He squats, his face pocked with holes. A girl approaches him with scissors. I recognize her. The girl clips a stem off a plant. It's called donkey tail, she says. Toss it in dirt and it will grow. The roots sprout pink. My grandson takes her hand and they start to leave. Make them stay. Are some plants poisonous? I shout my question and the girl lets go of Gabriel. She reaches toward me with strong arms. Under her fingernails there is dirt. With the scissors she cuts my hair. Slowly she turns into my mother. I shall be weeping this evening—

Wait.

It is warm under this blanket. Where am I? Alone in this bed. Where is my ex-husband? Dead these many years. There is the window and snow in the air and the waning moon. Teresa's book showed photographs of shot children. Crushed glass rubbed into chest wounds. Women's ribs. Men with legs folded like birds' wings. Decaying white bodies in piles.

Midnight now, and the snow grows. My nose is cold. My grandson Gabriel squats on the corner with pierced lips and swollen eyes. He is begging for money. Or dope. Who knows? The book showed Nazi women. Hitler's mistress holding a white rabbit and a sketch of herself. Mrs. Goebbels wandering like a ghost with cyanide in her bag. *I will feed it to them in hot chocolate.* Teresa thinks good is good and evil is bad. Her son is gone. Her husband Harry has gone prematurely gray.

My ex-husband, I tell the girl from the garden center, had cancer of the liver. She nods and says, Toss it in the earth and it will grow. You don't know what I mean, I say. What dope does my grandson take? Crystal meth? Acid? Cocaine? Heroin?

The girl wrinkles. She is Teresa in the mirror pinching her cheeks to make them glow. I shiver. The snow falls like an afghan. Daughter, I say, it is cold under this blanket. There is no dirt. Only asphalt and the concrete sidewalk under snow. The girl is gone. Snow falls like crystal powder and pluffs on the dirt. It lands on the backs of cars. On the backs of grandsons. On the backs of children and mothers. There in dimness I see the poinsettia black and gray. My trunk lies open. The closet is full of dark. The poinsettia sits in my room. Are some plants poisonous? My grandson Gabriel wanders like a ghost. Death waits at the door like a grandson.

Man in a Boat

MIKE GOOTEE'S my name. Or used to be. Last time I wrote it down. When Eve. When Eve and I. When I picked up my final paycheck from the Talbot County Correctional Facility, I'm sure I signed my name. Was that a Tuesday I retired from prison? Was it last Tuesday? Funny, now I'm breaking the law.

Stole this dinghy. Dragged it out of the Historical Society boathouse right onto this patchy ice.

Some black dude's coming down the bank of the Choptank. Walking in the snow. Jesus Christ, he's in all white. White derby. White overcoat. White trousers. White shoes. Mister, you gotta be kidding. Walking around Cambridge in a white suit, middle a December? I don't think so. Must not be from around here. Keep walking mister.

He won't see me out here on the ice.

It's sure cold on the river. I gotta get back inside. Except inside is cold too. I don't think the electric bills are right. They say I owe too much. Can't believe everything you read. In the paper today, I read about some kid's graffiti. Got it right here.

I lost a brother & with his spirit I converse daily & hourly in the Spirit

This graffiti kid copies old letters. Heard of William Blake? I never did. Listen to this. Kid paints this old poet's words on buildings in Baltimore. City pays him to do it.

I hear his advice & even now write from his Dictate—

Crazy old coot. Can't believe everything you read.

There's that black guy. Look at his pointy white collar. Crackpot. What's he doing? Way too damn dangerous to walk out on this river ice. Better stand back. What the hell is he doing?

& See him in my remembrance in the region of my Imagination

Wait, this can't be today's paper. Date on top says October, it's December, ain't it? Maybe it wasn't last week I signed my name. It was a Tuesday, though. Eve. Eve left me on a Tuesday. A couple months ago.

Is that guy walking out this way?

She said I was a dead end. I asked about our family. She said, what family, Mike Gootee? I said we should think on starting one. She said I was old and crazy. Sometimes I wished she would of been like other women, but then she wouldn't of been Eve.

This kid says Blake appears to him in dreams. I should copy one of his letters and mail it to Eve.

Eve. What happened to Eve? Before she left, she stopped. Stopped vacuuming. Stopped washing dishes. Stopped doing laundry. Just sat on the couch all day reading books. That was her sign. Preparing me. All's I read is the *Star-Republican*. I don't pay the bill, paper just keeps coming. She left on a Tuesday in December. Has it been a year already?

I should copy one of those letters and sign it with my name. Least what used to be my name. I think when Eve left she stole my name.

Maybe I'll call that dude out here. Ask if he'd like to ride on a stolen dinghy. Show him my paper. How this graffiti kid is in with spirits.

As to Myself about whom you are so kindly Interested, I live by Miracle

Why not?

He's walking away. What's he doing out in the middle a winter anyway?

"Hey! You in the white suit. I want to ask your mind on something."

He's pretty far away but he's turned. I can see his white hat. There's a couple holes in the brim.

"Hey," I yell again. "You ever read poetry?" Jesus, he's gonna think I'm queer. "I want to send a poem to someone. To remind her, know what I mean?"

I lean from my boat and reach toward him. Hold out the article showing the front page.

I really am sorry that you are falln out with the Spiritual World

He's nodding. Saying something. Walking this way on the ice. I can't quite hear him. His voice sounds, I don't know, like it's coming from far away.

"What's that?" I ask.

He's near me now. Right about to get in the boat. Dressed in a white derby. In the middle a December. White shoes. Hoyle. Hoyle? I think he's saying his name's Hoyle. He's dazzling. He's looking at the paper. Asking what I am called. He wants to know my name?

My wife is like a flame of many colours of precious jewels

"I think she took my name."

Thoughts

LAST APRIL, when we learned I was pregnant and moved up from Cambridge, Maryland, to Chris's home in Manhattan, I started thinking about my brain, the size and shape of it, how it works, whether I'll be satisfied with it after the baby comes.

Many unpleasant things happened that April and May. Sirens, spilled coffee, subway traffic, my job at JP Morgan, cold shoulders on walks home, grocery lines, Christopher not returning until nine, ten, eleven at night. My brain lay wide open, taking it all in, a funnel narrowing the flow to a single stream. It's amazing how calm and happy I felt thinking about the baby. My mother called every other day. Chris usually remembered in the morning to ask how I was feeling, pausing from his coffee at least for that. I might have gone crazy with loneliness if it weren't for my funnel.

Then at the start of summer I conceived of it differently. Instead of directing the flow, it lost most of the input. *Brain*, I doodled rather than taking notes during the investment meeting, = *sieve*. I wondered whether I had taken my vitamins. Whether I had turned off the bathroom light. Whether I had locked our apartment door. I watched the morning news, but I didn't remember what I saw by the time I arrived at work. At lunch I spoke with strangers, and on the occasion that Christopher and I saw each other in the evenings,

I couldn't remember what things anyone might have said. I looked out the tiny window in the kitchen at the purplish Manhattan skyline against the evening sky. I rubbed my enlarging middle and forgot about the cat needing food, the laundry service needing to be scheduled, the wedding gift thank-you notes still needing to be written. I forgot the names of Christopher's colleagues, the ones he met for drinks most nights. My sieve kept me quiet. New York and I both seemed to sleep with our eyes open, waiting for a smell, a sign, proof that something was wrong.

Then it was a spoon. I told my mother these ideas on the phone, and she laughed her *My daughter, silly girl!* laugh that helps her get along with her friends. A spoon stirs the pot. Chris was committed to his career, and I wanted to have a family. My mother didn't see any problem with the arrangement, that's how she and Father succeeded. *You call it success*, I stirred in my head. Last spring, a bride-to-be, I sent out the invitations my mother had had engraved, "Dr. William Snow and Mrs. Patricia Snow request the honor of your presence at the marriage of their daughter Sarah Elizabeth to Mr. Christopher Worthington Stone, Saturday, the twenty-first of February at Noon, Saint Andrew's Church, Cambridge, Maryland," and I spooned with Christopher every night until we conceived.

But by the end of the summer, one weekend Chris took off, and we walked together to Central Park, and we stood on the Lake at the Ladies' Pavilion, my brain finally became boat. For a moment, Chris seemed suddenly boyish, excited by my swollen middle after months of barely noticing. I felt giddy and confused, navigating through muddy waters. That's when my brain set a new course. Christopher went back to his extra hours at work, and my brain stayed afloat. I quit my job and floated through the city by myself. Battery Park, Rockefeller Center, the Empire State Building, the New York Public Library, the Manhattan Civil Courthouse. The last was a giant building, faced with limestone, and stainless steel, and a plaque that I stopped to read: "This courthouse was the City's first to be recognized and honored as barrier-free and accessible to persons with disabilities." I stepped up and waved my arms, and the automatic sensor didn't work. The glass doors stayed sealed. I moored myself there in the small park. A few days later, I packed my bag and pulled in the oars. I've drifted where the tide carried me, back to the Eastern Shore. Here I am in Cambridge, me and my brain and a baby about to be born.

Big Man

THAT THIN WOMAN is looking at us.

See her eyes running back and forth over our lines, girth, depth. Ow, Brucie buddy, you got to stop, we're stuck in a thick paste, you big ox. I'm not stuck. Yes you are, and that thin woman in black can tell. Remember her from the office? Dyed blond hair, narrow face, twitchy nose, sharp eyes. She's Frank's assistant. She's checking out our pink ears, our bags under our eyes. Don't look up! When she came in, there was snow on her black coat. She walked by our table once and now she's back with her pointed chin. Staring at our nose flesh, our flabby forearms, our hairless pate, oh geez. Suck it in, stop hulking. She's leaving now. Keep your nob down. Eyes on the page. Focus, read your book about Eva Braun. Why did she fall in love with Hitler?

We got to stop thinking this way. Yeah, and the North Dorchester Library should be built for fat people, Polyphemus.

Have we always been this way? No we have not. Once upon a time we were fine. We were a boy dreaming he might study history and psychology. We were alive with friends. We spent evenings at the Pub. We loved to sail on the Chesapeake. You weren't a temporary employee at Bishop Office Supply. You did not answer phones for a toady named Frank. You were unafraid of secretaries in black coats. What changed?

Peer around the room, black coat has disappeared. When she comes back, ask if she knows about Eva Braun, how she married her Adolf and the next day swallowed poison, and he shot himself in the head. How the books call her *plain* and *athletic*, but she was layered, concealing herself. Why'd she fall in love with a monster? black coat might ask. She was depressed, I'll say. She could not see well.

Here's Eva Anna Paula Braun. Look at this picture. Cute girl, but the books call her *plain* and *athletic*. Bruce, you got to find out what happened to Eva Braun. Why did she fall in love with a monster? It's not written down in history. If we could write poetry, we'd write about youth like a burned-down house. You're a kid again, Bruce, hitting a stitched white ball. You're running from first to second, sliding, eating dirt, scraping our hands, reaching, reaching, thrown out at third. You're in the home you grew up in, Dad riding his stationary bike, Mom reading *Tidewater Tales* on the couch. You are smoldering whitewash, streaked windows, and a smoky smell.

She's back. Walking across the waxy floor. Swiveling to stare at us. How do they know, these writers? What went on in private rooms? Braun was a photographer's assistant, that's documented. Of her life with Hitler they write, *She spent most of her time brooding, watching romantic films or concerning herself with her own appearance.* Bruce, look at yourself. When are you going to trim the hairs in your nose? My head hurts, a thick pressure like glue. Stop thinking this way. Eva Braun went to convent school, became Hitler's mistress, shot herself, didn't die. You sit here alone, Bruce, because you're huge. Because some small female dressed in black might find your body grotesque. You're naked, you're on display, you're the giant walrus at the zoo. *She spent most of her time exercising, reading cheap novelettes.* She tried again two years later with pills, didn't die, lived fourteen more years.

Oh God, there she is again, back with books, walking over to our table. We will not say a word. What has she chosen to read? Is she married? Kids? Don't have kids. In the bunker, Mrs. Goebbels killed all six of her children. Hitler believed geniuses could give birth to cretins. It makes a certain sense. Children are a risk. Dad taught psychology at Salisbury University, trim and fit, and Mom read all the time. I'm a whale working phones for a loser named Frank.

She's right behind you. We can hear her breath, shallow and light. Maybe she cannot speak. I should turn around. Focus, focus. Eva Braun was a blonde. The books call her *plain* and *athletic*, fond of skiing, gymnastics, and climbing mountains. I'm a big jellyroll. Is Frank's assistant still there? How do she and Frank get along? If I asked, she might answer, He's a bastard. I could nod, say, Known him for years. I don't plan on being there long, she'd say. She'd ask, What does someone like you like to read? I am two people, I'd say.

One crushing enormous elephant, who loves novels and psychology, and the other a history buff, as thin as a pane of glass.

Blind Boy

THE MOST BEAUTIFUL THING I know is the river stretching from Cambridge so far you lose sense of it. It runs to the Chesapeake Bay, then to the Atlantic Ocean, then away over the whole globe. My teacher Ms. Bowdle says water connects the continents, so Choptank water could show up anywhere on earth. Africa, Asia, Europe, anyplace you can name.

The other most beautiful thing is the color brown. Every time I like the way something feels, I'm told it's brown. My mother's hair is brown. My cat Henner is brown. The river is brown. Chocolate, walnuts, dogs in the park are brown. I like to dress in brown.

My cat Henner breathes on my windowsill. My mother sits with me on the sofa, watching out the apartment window and telling me what she sees. Solly, she says, There goes a man so large, his head looks like a big bald pillow, and he's not wearing a coat. What color is his shirt, I ask. Red, my mother tells me, apple red. What else, I ask. There goes a very pregnant lady, my mother says, in a mustard-colored coat, rubbing her belly around and around. Henner purrs softly on my arm. There is another cat who likes to sits on the sidewalk. My mother tells me he's pure white. He stares back at us, watching for Henner. Then he darts across the street, up the steps of another building, and stops to scratch. I wonder if he's out there now.

Henner sleeps with me at night. He tells the skeletons to go home. In my dreams, the skeletons tell me they are upset because they died before their time.

It's December 1, and not many families celebrate Hanukkah in Cambridge. Bobe, my father's mother, visits from Baltimore to light the menorah and sing *Shelo yichbe neiro l'olam v'ed.* Which means the light will burn forever. We give presents and spin dreidels, but before celebrating, we watch the documentaries. My father's grandparents, Johann and Ilse Katz, died at Auschwitz-Birkenau. Many cousins and great aunts and uncles of my father, at Treblin-ka and Dachau. My mother is not Jewish, she is from the Eastern Shore, but she manages the traditions. I sit by while she and Bobe grate potatoes. We eat latkes dipped in applesauce. *Shelo yichbe neiro l'olam v'ed.*

Every December, we watch the documentaries. We do this before Bobe arrives because she says it is a morbid thing to do. I agree that it is terrible. My father describes the pictures for me of six million people going to die. Barbed wire. Rows of wooden shoes. Signs with skull-and-crossbones. One film shows the American army sweeping through southern Germany. When the troops headed toward Hitler's headquarters, they found strange mounds in the snow. Every year, my father cries at the discovery of barely dressed people under a layer of snow. When the show ends, I hold my father's hand, and he puts me to bed. My cat is already on the blanket. My father kisses me goodnight.

Tucked in bed, I imagine the rough grain of wood on my feet. The smoothness of skulls. The cold skin of a body in snow. Some-times the people in the documentaries appear in my dreams, rising from the snow. They reach out with thin white fingers to touch my face. They look at me with big holes for eyes.

Then Henner arrives, all brown like a tree and a river, and he tells the people they are dead. Time to go home. He tells them to get out of my dreams. Sometimes the white cat comes, too. He and Henner feel the same color in my dream. They play and run in the snow.

I love to sit outside on the steps, but today everything is frozen, so Henner and I sit behind the windowpane. My mother tells me: There goes a man cradling a book, his coat is stuffed with newspaper. There goes a middle-aged woman with a camera, there are snowflakes stuck in her hair. There goes another woman with a tiny, tiny baby wrapped in fur, and she's holding the baby to her lips like you hold Henner.

Henner purrs. His friend the white cat watches from outside.

There are many things to love about winter. The crackling radiators at the library, the smell of wind off the frozen fields, my brown wool gloves and scarf that I wear out on the fishing bridge, my parents' voices as they describe the red and yellow sunset, the ice cracked by the tides. There are so many things. When I get old enough, I want to visit all the countries. Egypt, New Zealand, Brazil. I'll go to Germany and touch the barbed wire, the train tracks, the barracks, and the pits, and sunset-colored castles, and trains, and trails. Sometimes, in the winter, I touch the river ice that leads to the bay and out to the oceans. If it ever got cold enough, my sight could stretch over the whole world.

Mother

IN MY BELLY, on my belly—only minutes ago it was part of my body. I didn't imagine how its face would look like my father's, where's the nurse gone? A girl, the doctor said, I closed my eyes and saw a little dark moon. I opened and saw a reddish shriveled bump. What's her name, the doctor said, and I moaned, Eva Green. I can't touch this angry kitten humped on my front. The light is in my eyes, my legs are numb. Look at them shake. The thing on my belly is wet and apple-colored, the face of my father, only lighter skinned. I imagined it, and here it is, on my belly a huddled fish, a glistening hush, shocked to be loose from the womb. Flesh on flesh, her cord attached to me still. Not how I imagined it before. I had imagined something wavy and soft, wet inner flesh. There was a beat of two hearts, one fluttering fast, the other steady and slow, a song with no words. Inside me moments ago, she was a faceless, a kicking, a solid, supple mound. I'd imagined a dark huntress on a horse leaning into the world. Now I see something weak and knotty, gums and fuzz, mouth atremble. She is so separate now. Her mouth quavers in the angry mask of my father. My daughter Eva. What has she always already imagined before, when the world was a warm dark place? Before she crouched like a contracted muscle, color of plum, slippery and raw? What does she imagine now, helpless puddle on my belly? Does she imagine my face a mask of stone? I can't help it, I have become a mother, one of the world's dreams. A mother knows more than I know, a mother is warm and good. I am cold and fearful. I want to help this puzzled lump, this mouth about to bawl, but I am not strong. My legs are bowed, knees up to the ceiling, I can't feel them. My fists are exhausted balls. Where's the nurse gone, leaving this baby on my belly to wobble? What did I know before this, what was I, what happens now?

Rise

dedicated to Kati Kim

EIGHT DAYS, stuck in snow on a mountain. What do a woman and man say to one another? The saltines and cheese are gone, as well as pureed squash, sweet potato, and pear. They look at their seven-year-old and their baby wearing everything they'd packed for the trip. Emergency blankets line the windows and floors while the snow, continuing to fall, veils all the outdoors. The baby giggles to himself. The sound rises like helium to fill the station wagon. In the dim light of the front seat, they feel the weight of no answers. The moment lasts and lasts.

WHEN THEY'D STARTED OFF, the Smokies bore up on the horizon like giant ships. They drove northeast on the highway for several hours, catching glimpses, when Rachel looked at Tim and said, It would be nice to cut through the mountains. He nodded.

I'm hungry, Abigail complained. Rachel told her she could climb to the orange-colored cooler.

I don't like her taking off her seatbelt, Tim said.

Rachel, turning back, said, Wouldn't you love to see snow, Abby? They were heading north from a small Tennessee college back to their home in Maryland. Every reading made Tim nervous. Years before, Rachel had asked her husband whether with her there it was better or worse. It helps, he said. So Rachel always went, no matter how far, and now the children did too. At the reading she'd sat in the back, nursing the baby, Abigail occupied with Laura Ingalls Wilder. Tim read songlike passages from the end of his novel. The audience of mostly first-year students wore pained looks. To Rachel's left a girl played with her cell phone. *The falling out of hair, the loosening of skin, what would it mean to grow old together?* Tim read. *Who was she that I lived with? I'll sew a shroud of holland, every stitch a tear to run down cloth, and trim her hair strand by strand. Shorn birds fall then rise.* Rachel had heard these lines a hundred times. Tim's face was squared with stress. His eyes crossed hers with no particular recognition. That night in the hotel, with Abigail and Clement asleep on the other side of the room, they made love in quiet relief.

In the foothills the banks lay higher than Abigail's knee. I want to make angels, Abigail said, and Tim filmed her with the last of the camera's battery. Her red corduroy overalls flamed against the snow. In her matching wool hat, cheeks flushed, she waved through the car window to her baby brother. He laughed at the puffs of her breath on the glass. It did not start to snow until they were driving up a curling trail of switchbacks.

At a small pullover they gazed through gently falling flakes. The land, peaceful as an ocean, was broken by black and dark-green woods. Pretty, Rachel said.

The baby at nine months was quite good. He had pink cheeks and four teeth in his smile, and he slept through the night. Rachel and Tim did not know where he got his good nature—the rest of them, Abigail included, were prone to anxiety. It had taken them three weeks after his birth to settle on Clement, a funny name. When eating sweet foods he made the sound *di di*. He also said *taa*. Abigail said that meant Zeppelin, their cat. When the station wagon slid off the side of a shallow turn and ploughed into snow, its nose pointing up slightly like a shipwrecked bow, Clement emitted a soft *puh*.

Wow! Abigail said.

The car's rear was propped up on a sunken log. Rachel and Tim worked for hours. No shovel, so Tim tore the lid off the Rubbermaid cooler and scooped snow in heavy platefuls. Abby and Clement watched from the car. Rachel used her hands and two coffee mugs.

How far up did we come, Tim asked.

They guessed about fifteen miles.

There must be lots of people who drive this way, Rachel said.

How much snow was out there? They'd asked no questions before deciding on this mountain road. Had doubts started before or after the first slippery turn? Rachel wondered at the foot of snow balanced on fir tree boughs. Why hadn't they charged their cell phone, bought better tires? How good were other cars on one inch of snow, two inches? Was it getting worse? Was it going to stop?

As night fell they'd dug a path ten feet up to the road. They freed the car on its upward bank. Rachel got in the driver's seat, and Tim pushed. The wheels spun. Tim got back in the car. They were going nowhere in this sea of snow.

I need to piss, Tim said quietly.

Good timing, Rachel snapped.

He got back out of the car, muttering, What do you mean, good timing?

EIGHT DAYS, their car a small sunken island. What else can we do? he says. I have to go for help. She doesn't say, Why you? Hungry as a jackal after days on bits of ham and a jar of squash, her body still produces milk. They've filled the lidless cooler with snow that melts in the station wagon. There's still a half tank of gas. They've kept themselves warm even though the temperature outdoors drops below freezing at night. Drinking snow water in cardboard cups helps pass the time. They stare up at the ceiling, looking for answers. She whispers, Someone is coming. He shakes his head.

THEY TOOK QUICK BATHROOM TRIPS, yellowing an area just inside the tree line that each night's new snow covered. Dirty diapers piled in a snow heap behind the car. Dark trunks of deciduous trees stood watch, a few hemlocks and firs among them. Foraging, they found no pinecones, no berries. Tim picked some frozen grasses he insisted they could eat. Rachel collected branches and formed an SOS to be visible from the sky. The sign kept getting snowed out. In the mornings, small animal tracks, probably rabbits, or squirrels, punctuated the new snow.

In the car they sang songs. Old-MacDonald-Had-a-Farm. She'll-Be-Coming-Round-the-Mountain-When-She-Comes. They played rock, paper, scissors and read Clement's Margaret Wise Brown books. Rachel taught clapping games to Abigail and Tim. They read from *Little House in the Big Woods*. *The great, dark trees of the Big Woods stood all around the house,* he read, *and beyond them were other trees, and beyond them were more trees. As far as a man could go to the north in a day, or a week, or a whole month, there was nothing but woods.* They tried to keep their spirits up.

Clement slept in Rachel's arms. Abigail curled on Tim's lap. She started calling him *Pa.* I wish you'd named me Laura, she said. Can I call him Baby Carrie?

No, Rachel said.

She can call him whatever she wants, Tim said.

They slept or closed their eyes. When they woke, their stomachs whined and wailed, but on the surface they restrained themselves as best they could. The quiet seeped into their ears and kissed the insides. Dreams came of blackbirds splashing in a pedestal. Red and yellow balloons. Clement nursed. Abigail, not talking, blinked her eyes. They slept again, their breath rising in the car.

Before Tim left, Rachel saw his face sink. Eight days had gone by with no airplane, no helicopter, no rescue teams in bright sport uniforms. They spent the eighth night crying. Then lay in exhausted silence. Their last kiss was too short, and when Tim left the car, snow swirled around him. He stepped away purposefully, loaded with chosen belongings. Rachel saw something haphazard. Like a flock of birds leaving a field. He wore the black peacoat she had given him last Christmas. Turned and waved one mittened hand. Over Rachel's shoulder, Abigail bit her lip.

When's he coming back?

Sweetie, keep your hat on. It's only getting colder in here.

But it wasn't true. To Rachel's surprise the car warmed. Maybe as fear increased, their hearts beat hotter. Maybe the weather changed. Rachel nursed Clement, and between breasts he nuzzled. Then he slept, and Rachel and Abigail slept, too.

EIGHT DAYS passing, the snow twirls like white ferns. Together they plan a trail of clues for him to sow, pointing from the car like a vector. The empty orange cooler. Leave it on the road. The baby's blue car seat. Prop it on snow at the first ridge. Pages from the atlas. Hang them on tree branches. Little red overalls saved as a last sign, in case...in case.... They write a letter for him to carry. Choosing each word takes an eternity. He sets his book, *Who was she* and *Shorn birds fall* on the dashboard. His eyes are brown and hers grey—they know this moment by heart. *The falling out of hair, the loosening of skin, what would it mean to grow old together?* the story goes.

AFTER HE LEFT, more snow fell. Running or reading or gardening, in a world with such things, Rachel had on occasion forgotten she was a mother. It felt like an empty balloon whooshing back to groundedness brought on by her daughter and son. But she'd never had moments of forgetting Tim. He was as basic to her as skin.

Now he was out there stamping through snow, breaking a trail, being blanketed. He would drink from the bottle inside his jacket, fill it again and again with snow. Trudge back and forth from peace to panic. She imagined him surrounded by blankness. Climbing and planting evidence of their family in clearings visible to the sky.

What if he meets a panther? Abigail asked.

Her eyes reminded Rachel of a cat's. Sometimes back home, looking into Zeppelin's eyes, Rachel knew the cat was smarter than she.

From her lap, Clement batted her face then nursed and slept again. The light coming through the shadowy trees lessened until they sat in the dark. Rachel dreamt the world was a body. The car a belly. The woods swallowed the car and snow pumped around it like blood. Tire, bumper, hood. Tim and she were forty-one—she thought of fatalities people faced. Heart disease, stroke, brain cancer. In the car held by snow and trees, Rachel and the children waited. Rachel could not slow like time. She nursed Clement again and again.

He's going to be okay, she repeated.

I'm hungry, Mom.

For days the sun shone and the weather was warm, Rachel read. *There was no frost on the windows in the mornings. All day the icicles fell one by one from the eaves with soft smashing and crackling sounds in the snowbanks beneath.* While she read about sugar snow, she pictured Abigail's empty corduroys laid on a ridge like a bloody angel.

She said to her daughter, Don't you wish we had syrup?

Abigail was quiet.

We could eat away all the snow if we had syrup, Rachel said to make her daughter smile.

Rachel herself could not imagine the end of snow. In her memory, snow suffused their home. Zeppelin hunted flakes falling in the kitchen. From the snowy table in his nursery, Clement's underarms lifted yellow-pink. Tim's breath on her cheek coldly puffed. Abigail's brown hair on the pillow smelled like snow.

Goodnight moon, Abigail said.

She curled against Rachel's side and didn't say anything more.

EIGHT DAYS passing, the snow swims like white fish. They sit and debate. To move or stay put. If they wait longer they'll lose all strength. They fold and unfold the map a thousand times. These lines mean snowmobile trails? Here a tiny black speck denotes a house? Hard to read answers in the map. If I don't find anyone, I return. How do you get back, if you go far? I promise. They peer through the shadows of branches and trunks. They each look in the other's eyes and then away—the moment can't last forever but does. How much distance will you cover? What will you do if I don't return? Hard to read, love.

THE SUN ROSE through the dark trees. Rachel listed all the dangers outside. Ice crusts giving way to rocks. Laden branches dropping their loads. Impassable rivers where before had been creeks. Inside on her lap, Clement rested, a warm ball. He was swaddled in a dirty towel. Abigail slept across the seat with her hands folded against Rachel's thigh. In silent wonder, Clement looked on his sister and reached for her hair.

She'll be up soon, Rachel whispered to the baby.

Tim had been gone two days, and Rachel's milk was coming less and less. This morning before sunrise, she had woken knowing what to do.

She said loudly, Abigail. Clement smiled as if he smelled warm bread.

Abigail moaned and rubbed and opened her eyes. What, said her eyes.

I need you to drink some milk. I'll show you how.

Rachel moved Clement to her side, hugging him with one arm.

Abigail climbed over Rachel's leg to kneel on the car floor. Rachel unbuttoned her nipple at her daughter's mouth. She expressed thin streams, and Abigail swallowed. The girl leaned forward, eyes shut, and nursed until Rachel's breast was empty. Rachel touched her daughter's cheek. Helped her shift to the other side.

Over the morning, Rachel nursed Abigail twice more. They waited for the sun's warmest hours. At noon, she opened the car door.

Today we're going to walk like Daddy did.

Her voice floated out the door as if tethered. They wobbled when they stood, and Rachel's arms shook. For a moment, she wished to be swallowed by the snow rather than step away from Tim's and her car.

We can do this.

She lifted Clement from the back seat and walked ten steps toward the road. Their station wagon looked like a shiny metal rowboat upturned. Snow had melted away. Anyone who saw it might think of summer, maybe a lake nearby. Who would envision the real thing, a family surviving inside? Rachel remembered something, part of Tim's and her plan.

Abigail, hold the baby.

The girl's head bobbed atop its piling. Rachel set Clement upright in Abigail's arms. When she reentered the front seat, the stench rushed at her. Sweat, urine, feces, hunger, fear. Her head swam. She reached for Tim's book. Rip out pages or write inside? She took the pencil and opened to the inner back cover. *I have our children in the snow heading down. Husband went up. Help.* She tucked the open book in the dash. Outside, Abigail clung to the bundle that was her little brother. Rachel left the car like a shred of hope.

We're shipping out, she told her children.

Abigail shivered, dark moons under her eyes, red hat pulled low. Rachel took the baby. They walked, the snow's crust holding each footstep for a moment and then caving. Abigail went first. The up-and-down movement made her look like a fluttering flag. Rachel told her to go behind. Carrying Clement, Rachel gave up the effort to stand on the surface. She simply broke trail, each step pushing through snow deep in places to her waist.

In the short spaces between breaths, Rachel heard it. A rumble, a whine. Maybe the cracking of trees, smashing of snow. As if some machine far off were making its way up or through the mountain.

Did Abigail hear?

A glance at the girl's pale face told her no. This was wishful, a wishful thinking. Rachel's heart sped. They went one hundred feet from the car and dropped down. Just for a moment—Rachel knew they couldn't stop. They had to keep walking. She set Clement on the snow and sank. Abigail sank beside her, legs and arms shaking.

Then it was louder. From Abigail's thin chest came a sound, a rusty nail call like a blackbird's. Rachel moved one hand from Clement's body to touch Abigail, who jumped upward and swept off her red hat. A yellow roof and windshield appeared over a snowbank. Headlights like discerning eyes, balloons, wings cutting the air. The eyes looked at the sunken car and dark wood of the trees on the snow, and Rachel watched her daughter wave her red hat, up and up. Later, she would shed a river of tears, sew a shroud of holland, collapse for days on end. Now, she would follow her daughter. She clutched the baby and pushed one hand down against the snow so they could rise.

Unfinished Stories of Girls

I. Cats under the Bay

You want to hear the story of cats who live in the Chesapeake, love? Once upon a time there was an ugly girl named Rose, who had short hair that stuck out like straw, and a nose that pointed sideways like an arrow, while her cheekbones were bold and high—but we need to tell about Marie first, love. You need to know about the girl who was a sweet little child like you, whose hair was rich and curly, who had a dimpled chin, whose eyes were periwinkle blue. She bit her fingernails, her only flaw, and that's because her mother died when she was small, and her Daddy couldn't care for cows and chickens and a baby besides, and they struggled along until Marie was ten, and the money ran out. What do I do? moaned her father. Little Marie didn't know. She brought him tea with warm milk. That's what you would do for your Daddy, wouldn't you, love?

II. We Are Pretty Sure

Don't you want to know the story of cats under the bay? Once upon a time there was a girl named Marie, a good, sweet child like you, her hair rich and curly, her eyes aqua blue, her fingernails bitten, and that's because her mother had died and Daddy couldn't care for cows and chickens and a baby besides, and they struggled along, and their money ran out, and Daddy said, What do I do? and little Marie didn't know, and Daddy found another woman to marry, one with a cruel daughter named Rose.

III. Say Something Supernatural

ONCE UPON A TIME, sweet little Marie with hair as brown as mahogany, liquid eyes, and a cute, dimpled chin, whose mother died when she was small, brought her Daddy tea with warm milk, and he married a cruel and selfish woman who brought along her own daughter named Rose. Think of an old wooden spoon, love. When little Marie was late milking their three cows, the stepmother whacked her with the spoon, and Rose, older by a year, got to whack her , too. Every day they beat her silly, hitting her on the back of the head, so her father couldn't see the bruises. She didn't speak out until she was all alone, head aching, crying into the sky for her mother. The moon, when it appeared, hung low and pushy. No one ever answered. Even working from sunrise to sundown, Daddy and the stepmother and the two daughters couldn't make ends meet. The eggs and garden and milk from the cows wouldn't buy enough flour and cloth and oil. After a few years more, Daddy left to go up north, hoping to send back money. The stepmother and Rose continued the sweeping of floors, folding of clothes, finding of eggs. Someone had to fill in for Daddy, so it was little Marie who chased cows out of the poison ivy and greenbriers, who choked on ashes sweeping out the chimney, who chopped fallen oak and beech wood and blistered her hands. Late one afternoon, when it was time to stop working, the stepmother handed the little girl a large basket. It could have been filled with rocks, it was so heavy. Down to the water, the stepmother ordered. Do this laundry, and back before dark. She whacked Marie on the temple and slammed the door. The winter sun swayed over the western shore, and frost glassed the rocks leading to the bay. The little girl walked a few steps and collapsed under a crabapple tree. She whispered, Mother. This time, in the shadows cast by the tree, a voice answered. Love, it said, Go down to the bay and wash the clothes. When Marie looked up at the moon, it winked.

IV. *Enter the Wise Old Woman*

AS YOU MIGHT GUESS, little Marie carried the basket down to the water, and found the sun lining the water from over on the western shore. The line from the sun pointed at Marie, or maybe it pointed away, as she knelt on the breaker rocks. She dipped in her hands, and her knuckles froze, and her bit of soap slipped into the bay. Her only soap! She plunged her arm in up to the shoulder, but it was no good, the soap was gone. She buried her face in her cold, wet hands. A touch, light as a dragonfly, caused Marie to turn and see a tiny old woman standing beside her. She wore a stained apron over a blue gingham dress. Her white hair breathed out vanilla. In her arm was a cane, layered with circus animals, carousel creatures, seagulls with perch scales, and crabs with mosquito wings, and deer with human hands. What are you looking for, love? the old woman cackled. Excuse me, gulped the girl. She wiped her nose with the back of her hand. I lost something in the water, she said. The old woman nodded. Well jump in and look for it, the old woman grinned. Jump in? Wouldn't the water freeze her to death? Was this what her mother would want her to do? How could she breathe? What was down there besides her soap? Marie started to ask, but the old woman was gone. The only hint of her was the sound of her cane tapping the rocks. The sun slipped below the western horizon, and Marie shivered and put her thumbnail between her teeth. The bay shimmered like black ice. Marie could see the reflections of stars, points of light like baby's breath, twinkling in the water. Maybe they were a reflection, maybe an invitation, love. In she dove.

V. I Always Dreamed I Could Breathe Underwater

DO YOU REMEMBER me telling you this story before? About Marie, lovely Marie, wiping her tears, and talking to the old woman, and diving into the Chesapeake Bay? The water, cold as snow, filled her ears. Under the water the girl's body started to tingle. She couldn't hold her breath for long. But as she descended, the water lightened in density and softened like a cloud. Marie opened her eyes as she sank through an umbrella of jellyfish. She saw that she was growing warmer, and the water brightening, the color of sunflowers, more and more transparent. Fish swooped like field swallows, and seaweed floated and bobbed. A swirl of bubbles surrounded her, and she opened her mouth and breathed! She inhaled an orange glow. Hundreds of feet down, lights twinkled like a string of ships. She passed through that layer of lights, hanging like necklaces in the upper currents, and below her, bright as day, roads and farms wove as in a maze, the center of which was a massive tree. The giant tree, love, was a sea elm, its branches so sturdy and wide they could be walked on. Where Marie landed, the branch led some distance to a strange building, a turreted castle, nestled in the tree's trunk. Golden pickerel and bass swam in and out of windows. An ivory doorway shone. A shadow-colored cat sat before the gate, its whiskers and ears twitching at the golden fish. Marie, drawing close, wondered if he'd been locked outside, or whether his job was to guard the tree-castle door. He seemed to be talking to himself.

VI. Is This Supposed to Be About Our Life?

THE SHADOW OF A CAT at the gate looked up as the girl approached. I need help, she said, I've lost my soap.

Mom?

Don't interrupt, love—

Can you teach me how to talk to cats?

VII. The Moral of the Story

JUST LISTEN NOW. The little girl asked about her soap, and the gray porter raised its whiskers like someone lifting a curtain, and Marie heard it say, Follow me. The cat's tail swished like the girl's hair, and tickled her nose as she followed the cat through the gate down a hallway of open doors. She peered into a large room with a chandelier of shells and mosaic floors. A dining table in the center was set for a party, and a small black cat dusting a mussel-trimmed mantel, stretched the whole length of its body to reach, looking as if it were about to fall. Marie cried, Let me help! Taking the cat's seaweed brush, she swept the mantel and giant-clam chairs. To reach the chandelier she lifted the black cat to her shoulders. It purred and purred, and out in the hall, the porter raised its whiskers. After the watery dust was gone, they continued their walk past silver lanterns and vases full of arrowheads and sunken colonial coins. Passages glowed with bay pearls, the likes of which Marie had never seen. A tawny cat folded sheets in another room, and Marie could not resist calling, Let me. The cat held two corners, and they smoothed the wrinkles. The porter didn't say a word, just kept taking new turns past walls of stone coral and kelp, oyster sculptures on pedestals encrusted with mother-of-pearl, cup corals flowering on limestone urns. One hall turned into another. Marie helped a dozen cats. A white cat sponging up floors. A tabby kneading dough. A calico with a broom.

Mom, this isn't what I need. Do you have anything more to say?

VIII. Theory of Paracelsus: What Makes a Man Ill Also Cures Him
PAY ATTENTION, love. Deep underwater, in the center of the palace, there was a purple cushion atop a brain coral throne. The seat overlooked a high-ceilinged ballroom with bird's nest coral chandeliers, and every evening after the palace meal, all the cats would come to the throne room to dance. They danced waltzes and polkas, reels and jigs, and sometimes they danced something all their own, that no humans have ever seen. As soon as messengers brought the King news of the land girl, he asked his heralds to announce a special ball, so as the porter cat brought Marie to enter the ballroom, the cat dancers lined the walls. The girl looked around in wonder. She screamed when the King pounced down from his throne. Long, silver fur flowed around his chest. His yellow eyes shone like bulbs. When he asked, What are you looking for, girl? his question was

fifty cats mewing at the same time. Marie shook from head to foot.

Were you ever confused, Mom?

What are you talking about?

About Dad, about my brothers and sisters, about me. I need to know.

Rowwrr, the King said with so many voices to Marie. Your highness, Marie curtsied, I've come to ask— Don't worry about the soap, he said, More to the point, do you dance? The tribe of cats formed a line. The King opened his arm and nodded to the musicians. A small white cat with a baton announced, Constellation Square!

IX. Dirty Dancing

CAN I TELL IT? *Back in her town, the girl had seen all the dances you've told me about. The Dixie Twirl, the Devil's Dream, the Settlement Swing. She reached out and took the King's paw, and the King danced her around the floor, and she followed his steps. In her memory, her mother was alive and well, and she remembered how her mother had once held her father. Marie and the King twirled through the bay air and through Catdom, and when she began to tire, seven kittens came along with the purple cushion and lifted her onto it, and the poor girl looked down at her stained dress, and the dirt under her fingernails. I think I understand, Mom.*

What do you understand? Did you know your father was a wonderful dancer? You never saw him dance. The Push and Shove. Shoot the Moon. The best Roll in the Hay anyone ever saw. My sister was the dancer in our family. It was beautiful to watch those two. You ask someday, see what he admits.

Did you and Dad...?

I can't dance to save my life.

X. Listen, Be a Good Girl

IN THE BALLROOM, wearing her old worn dress, with her short, cracked fingernails, the little girl floated in the air that was the bay. After she felt rested, the seven kittens lowered her to the mosaic floor, and there sat her basket of laundry, fresh and soft and clean as cooked cream. Beside it, the King gazed. Time to rise, he mewed. *Already?*

You don't want the story to end? I can slow it down, love. Marie was a pretty, good girl, a sweet little child like you, and she wanted to stay under the bay, but no one can do that. The King put a paw to her cheek. He brushed her lips with his whiskers. They took a few more turns to music that rolled and whirred, twirled and swam. Finally, the King bowed again, and touched his wet nose to the back of her hand, and said once more, Time to rise. He said to the porter, Take her to the mirror so she can see. The porter nodded, and Marie hugged the King goodbye. Back through the hallways she followed the porter past fifty silver mirrors to a halt, inside the final gate, where stood a reflection as tall as Marie herself. The porter pointed toward it. He was as silent as a perch. Marie stared inside, and Marie-in-the mirror looked back, eyes full of water. Behind her in the mirror, she saw Rose and the stepmother crouched in front of the hearth, and three animals sat on three chairs. First, the King, who bowed his head. Second, a matte-brown donkey, chewing a straw. Third, a rooster with a crimson tail. Marie saw herself in the mirror wearing a gown, her eyes closed, rising through water like a bubble. The mirror-Marie's eyes stayed closed when the donkey brayed. They opened when the rooster crowed, and something bright and lovely flew up from the rooster's wing. Before Marie could ask what it meant, the porter opened the palace gate. With a swish of his tail, he sent her flying up through the bay. The currents rushed across her cheeks and lids. A rooster crowed as if to awaken the sun, and Marie opened her eyes and saw stars and the pie-faced moon and was herself again, on the hillside bank, resting on a bed of old fishing nets. Beside her sat the basket of laundry and, atop it, a new block of soap. The night was bright. Draped in green silk, the girl climbed the rocks to the road. A carriage waited, trimmed in mother-of-pearl, with two whiskered footmen who took the basket from Marie's arms and ushered her inside.

But, Mom.

What is it now?

This isn't the right story.

What makes a story right or wrong? It's a story!

XI. Miasms

BACK AT THE HOUSE the girl's stepmother and ugly sister Rose lay fast asleep. Marie tiptoed to the bed, and tapped her stepmother's shoulder. The mean woman shuddered awake. Stepmother, I visited a castle, Marie whispered, where cats washed our clothes. What's that on your face? the stepmother snapped. At that, ugly Rose awoke. She stumbled out of bed and leaned like a broom on the far wall and saw, on Marie's forehead, a sparkling flower of a diamond. She heard Marie tell her tale from the beginning, about the dance, the King, the purple cushion, the mirrors, the rooster. Ugly Rose watched her mother inspect the jewel on Marie's forehead. Marie said, They washed all our clothes, they gave me a carriage—

Mom?

You know, love, I did leave out part of the story. I have to go back again.

XII. I Wanna Be Your Lover

LET ME HELP, *Mom, that part you missed. Let me tell it.*

Someone else saw the little girl appear from the bay. A boy, the prince of a neighboring county, was sitting on the cliff. He watched Marie awaken on the fishing net hillock. He gazed as she picked up the basket and climbs into the carriage. He didn't know where she'd come from, so he followed.

This prince of another county listens at the window as Marie tells her stepmother everything that has happened, and when the stepsister, Rose, glances up at the window, she catches sight of the handsome boy. Rose stares at the prince, but suddenly the stepmother grabs her by the hair and drags her from the room.

Yes, love. Men fall in love just like that.

I'm talking about Rose, Mom. But then she's gone, and Marie, shocked by what her stepmother has just done, hears someone whistle. The prince is standing at the window. She look into his eyes, and wonderful, they're in love, he's saying he will take her far from this place, and she agrees to live in his county. But her stepmother returns with the spoon. Who is this boy with Marie? The stepmother is so stunned that at first she can't move. The stranger is reaching through the window, Marie is clasping his hands, the stepmother trips on a floorboard, and spits, and hisses. Marie clambers away. She marries the prince, and they live—

XIII. Bad Girl

YOU FORGOT about the ugly girl, my love. Where was Rose? Locked out of the house, watching the prince hand Marie into the carriage and roll down the road, the prince and her sister, and what could she do now? Run after them? Beg for their help? No! What are you waiting for? her mother screamed. You heard the story, so go down the hill and jump into the bay and find this King of cats! And Rose did as her mother said. The old woman appeared and told Rose to go down into the bay. But a terrible jealousy gnawed Rose's insides, and the lights dizzied her as she sank. She banged at the ivory door, and the porter cat could smell the bitterness on her like mud.

Through the halls Rose tripped, stepping on the porter's tail. When does the dancing start? she asked. How do I get out of this place? Messengers sent word to the King, and when Rose arrived in the hall, the King held up one paw. His whiskers shivered. He could see that the girl was just a young thing. Look into those mirrors, he mewed, pointing down the hall, And tell us what you see. Rose stomped to a mirror and stared. Where were the dancers? The music? The purple settee? She turned to report to the King, but which had come first? The rooster or the dirty brown ass? When do I get new clothes? she blurted. You misunderstand, my dear, the King said. He said, Here you dress yourself. Rose rocketed upward, as if to a whole new universe. Her eyes blurred. A rooster crowed in her mother's tongue, and Rose thought she was being tricked, so she kept her eyes clamped shut, while at the donkey's bray, the noise of twelve boys crying, she threw a glance backward over her shoulder to see yellow teeth in a laughing mouth. Next thing she knew, she lay on the hillside next to a basket of old wet clothes, in her lap, a scab of soap. She rubbed her eyes. Her fingers met something rough. She bent over the water, her eyes cleared, and she saw that a donkey's tail had sprouted right in the middle of her forehead.

The end.

That is not how it ends.

XIV. Homeopathy

ONCE UPON A TIME *a sister, often told that she was a good girl, traveled to an underwater world and helped a bunch of cats and got a jewel on her forehead and met a boy and fell in love, and the cats still live under the bay. Another sister, ugly, went under the bay and got an awful tail. So she tried to leave. She met people and invented lies about how the tail got on her forehead.*

Once her chest didn't hurt so badly, she started to tell the truth. She hadn't paid attention to a King and his coded messages and therefore got this tail-thing. One day, she knocked on her sister's door. Her sister, the diamond on her forehead shining but sore to the touch, welcomed her. Come live with me and my husband and our little daughter, she said. Sometimes one sister's tail hurt, and other times it didn't, and sometimes the other sister's forehead scratched, and sometimes it oozed pus. For years, the sisters took care of each other.

Finally, the sister with the tail moved out to a lighthouse, where she always welcomed her niece. The little niece didn't even notice her aunt's donkey tail, not really, she was so used to it, until one day, when she reached up to touch it, it fell off. The end.

The end?

Well, Mom, their father, who'd been missing a long time and knew nothing about cats under the Chesapeake, returned with a sack of riches and a head full of trouble. He couldn't find his wife. He couldn't find their children either. He climbed down a cliff to look out at the water, where an old woman on the shore suggested that he dive in. Was she crazy? Out there, something bobbed. His wife? It was his wife, he thought. He started swimming, and he's out there, still. The bay won't let him swim all the way. He and his wife, if it is his wife, survive on scraps dropped by gulls. To this day the daughters come and visit and they bring others, and everyone tells stories, and sometimes people hike up and down the rocky shore, listening for the tap-tapping of an old woman's cane.

Acknowledgements

This book could not have found a more phenomenal editor than Marc Estrin. My thanks to him and Donna Bister of Fomite for their guidance at every turn, and for their marriage of political activism and beautiful, strange books. It has also been an honor to work with designer Kurt Volk, whose talents make me want to dance. And it is my greatest privilege to share these pages with the artist Ann Piper, with whose art these stories now get to be in endless conversation.

Thanks to the literary magazine editors who have worked with me, including Roxanne Gay, Maria Mazziotti Gillan, Kim Long, Sena Jeter Naslund, Christina Thompson, and Grant Tracey; and to Allison Joseph, Jon Tribble, and Charles Johnson, who gave me a vote of confidence when I was a student writer; and to the writers who have supported this book: Michael Cocchiarale, Rebecca Godwin, Ann Pancake, Steven Yarbrough, and Claire Vaye Watkins. The poets and novelists of Shippensburg University—Kazim Ali, John Taggart, Kim van Alkemade, and Catherine Wing—shared their breath when I needed it, and my Susquehanna colleagues Tom Bailey, Gary Fincke, Karla Kelsey, and Glen Retief provide daily inspiration. All my gratitude to the brilliant students who read these stories and offered their feedback, Melissa Bierly, Dana Diehl, Jennifer Farina, and Melissa Goodrich, and to my spirited book publicist, Megan Kaufenberg. And to Joseph Scapellato, who has been a constant friend.

I think often of my Binghamton University mentors, Susan Strehle, Jack Vernon, Jaimee Wriston-Colbert, and Joe Church, and of intense collaborative studies with Letitia Moffitt and Jacob White, and of workshops and friendships with fellow graduate students Giselda Beaudin, Beth Couture, Adrianne Finlay, Maggie Gerrity, Andy Famiglietti, Kathy Henion, Deborah Poe, and Jeremy Schraffenberger. I tribute John Barth for writing about the mythological land of my childhood in a way that made me think and laugh, and Margaret Atwood for writing new gender mythology, and Lydia Davis whose graciousness over the years is its own mythology. I'm grateful to all the people from Talbot and Dorchester Counties, including Phoebe Cuppett-Caverly, Tom Flowers, Brian Barnes, Susan LaMotte, Susan Patterson, Margaret B. Thompson, Gilda Sadoff, Nancy Andrew, Edmund Coppinger, Midge Fuller, Ellen General, John General, Julie Heikes, Michael Valliant, who helped me see my way from the muddy banks.

To my beloved parents, my brothers, and all my family and friends on the Eastern Shore and elsewhere: thank you.

Ann Lockhart and Adrienne Dent commented on these stories in embryonic form, and their discernment and understanding is so appreciated.

I thank my children Emerson and Lake forever for their love. Their father, Silas Dent Zobal, taught me to pay attention to language and forms, and his insight is felt on every page of my life.

ABOUT THE AUTHOR

CATHERINE ZOBAL DENT was born in Washington, D.C., and raised on Maryland's Eastern Shore. Her fiction has appeared in *Harvard Review, North American Review, PANK,* and other print and online journals. While at Binghamton University in 2006, she won the Charles Johnson Award for Student Fiction. She is the fiction and poetry editor of *Modern Language Studies* and an Assistant Professor at the Writers Institute of Susquehanna University. This is her debut story collection.

About the Artist

ANN PIPER was born in New London, Connecticut. She earned a BFA from the Maryland Institute College of Art and an MFA from New Mexico State University. Her paintings and drawings have been exhibited widely across the United States for the past fifteen years. Her work has appeared in numerous publications, including *The Perception of Appearance: A Decade of American Contemporary Figurative Drawing* (Frye Art Museum, Seattle, Washington) and the *4th International Painting Annual* (MANIFEST, Cincinnati, Ohio). She has received various awards and honors, such as the Roswell Artist-in-Residence Grant and the Kansas Arts Commission Fellowship Award. Currently, she is an Associate Professor of Studio Art at Susquehanna University.

IMAGE TITLES

Fomite
Burlington, VT

A fomite is a medium capable of transmitting infectious organisms from one individual to another.

"The activity of art is based on the capacity of people to be infected by the feelings of others." Tolstoy, *What Is Art?*

Flight and Other Stories - Jay Boyer

In *Flight and Other Stories*, we're with the fattest woman on earth as she draws her last breaths and her soul ascends toward its final reward. We meet a divorcee who can fly with no more effort than flapping her arms. We follow a middle-aged butler whose love affair with a young woman leads him first to the mysteries of bondage and then to the pleasures of malice. Story by story, we set foot into worlds so strange as to seem all but surreal, yet everything feels familiar, each moment rings true. And that's when we recognize we're in the hands of one of America's truly original talents.

Loisaida - Dan Chodorokoff

Catherine, a young anarchist estranged from her parents and squatting in an abandoned building on New York's Lower East Side, is fighting with her boyfriend and conflicted about her work on an underground newspaper. After learning of a developer's plans to demolish a community garden, Catherine builds an alliance with a group of Puerto Rican community activists. Together they confront the confluence of politics, money, and real estate that rule Manhattan. All the while she learns important lessons from her great-grandmother's life in the Yiddish anarchist movement that flourished on the Lower East Side at the turn of the century. In this coming-of-age story, family saga, and tale of urban politics, Dan Chodorkoff explores the "principle of hope" and examines how memory and imagination inform social change.

Improvisational Arguments - Anna Faktorovich

Improvisational Arguments is written in free verse to capture the essence of modern problems and triumphs. The poems clearly relate short, frequently humorous, and occasionally tragic stories about travels to exotic and unusual places, fantastic realms, abnormal jobs, artistic innovations, political objections, and misadventures with love.

Carts and Other Stories - Zdravka Evtimova

Roots and wings are the key words that best describe the short story collection *Carts and Other Stories*, by Zdravka Evtimova. The book is emotionally multilayered and memorable because of its internal power, vitality and ability to touch both your heart and your mind. Within its pages, the reader discovers new perspectives and true wealth, and learns to see the world with different eyes. The collection lives on the borders of different cultures. *Carts and Other Stories* will take the reader to wild and powerful Bulgarian mountains, to silver rains in Brussels, to German quiet winter streets, and to wind-bitten crags in Afghanistan. This book lives for those seeking to discover the beauty of the world around them, and will have them appreciating what they have—and perhaps what they have lost as well.

Fomite
Burlington, VT

Zinsky the Obscure - Ilan Mochari

"If your childhood is brutal, your adulthood becomes a daily attempt to recover: a quest for ecstasy and stability in recompense for their early absence." So states the 30-year-old Ariel Zinsky, whose bachelor-like lifestyle belies the torturous youth he is still coming to grips with. As a boy, he struggles with the beatings themselves; as a grownup, he struggles with the world's indifference to them. *Zinsky the Obscure* is his life story, a humorous chronicle of his search for a redemptive ecstasy through sex, an entrepreneurial sports obsession, and finally, the cathartic exercise of writing it all down. Fervently recounting both the comic delights and the frightening horrors of a life in which he feels—always—that he is not like all the rest, Zinsky survives the worst and relishes the best with idiosyncratic style, as his heartbreak turns into self-awareness and his suicidal ideation into self-regard. A vivid evocation of the all-consuming nature of lust and ambition—and the forces that drive them.

Kasper Planet: Comix and Tragix - Peter Schumann

The British call him Punch; the Italians, Pulchinella; the Russians, Petruchka; the Native Americans, Coyote. These are the figures we may know. But every culture that worships authority will breed a Punch-like, anti-authoritarian resister. Yin and yang—it has to happen. The Germans call him Kasper. Truth-telling and serious pranking are dangerous professions when going up against power. Bradley Manning sits naked in solitary; Julian Assange is pursued by Interpol, Obama's Department of Justice, and Amazon.com. But—in contrast to merely human faces— masks and theater can often slip through the bars. Consider our American Kaspers: Charlie Chaplin, Woody Guthrie, Abby Hoffman, the Yes Men—theater people all, utilizing various forms to seed critique. Their profiles and tactics have evolved along with those of their enemies. Who are the bad guys that call forth the Kaspers? Over the last half century, with his Bread & Puppet Theater, Peter Schumann has been tireless in naming them, excoriating them with Kasperdom....*from Marc Estrin's Foreword to Planet Kasper*

The Co-Conspirator's Tale - Ron Jacobs

There's a place where love and mistrust are never at peace; where duplicity and deceit are the universal currency. *The Co-Conspirator's Tale* takes place within this nebulous firmament. There are crimes committed by the police in the name of the law. Excess in the name of revolution. The combination leaves death in its wake and the survivors struggling to find justice in a San Francisco Bay Area noir by the author of the underground classic *The Way the Wind Blew: A History of the Weather Underground* and the novel *Short Order Frame Up*.

Short Order Frame Up - Ron Jacobs

1975. America as lost its war in Vietnam and Cambodia. Racially tinged riots are tearing the city of Boston apart. The politics and counterculture of the 1960s are disintegrating into nothing more than sex, drugs, and rock and roll. The Boston Red Sox are on one of their improbable runs toward a postseason appearance. In a suburban town in Maryland, a young couple are murdered and another young man is accused. The couple are white and the accused is black. It is up to his friends and family to prove he is innocent. This is a story of suburban ennui, race, murder, and injustice. Religion and politics, liberal lawyers and racist cops. In *Short Order Frame Up*, Ron Jacobs has written a piece of crime fiction that exposes the wound that is US racism. Two cultures existing side by side and across generations--a river very few dare to cross. His characters work and live with and next to each other, often unaware of each other's real life. When the murder occurs, however, those people that care about the man charged must cross that river and meet somewhere in between in order to free him from (what is to them) an obvious miscarriage of justice.

Fomite
Burlington, VT

All the Sinners Saints - Ron Jacobs

A young draftee named Victor Willard goes AWOL in Germany after an altercation with a commanding officer. Porgy is an African-American GI involved with the international Black Panthers and German radicals. Victor and a female radical named Ana fall in love. They move into Ana's room in a squatted building near the US base in Frankfurt. The international campaign to free Black revolutionary Angela Davis is coming to Frankfurt. Porgy and Ana are key organizers and Victor spends his days and nights selling and smoking hashish, while becoming addicted to heroin. Police and narcotics agents are keeping tabs on them all. Politics, love, and drugs. Truths, lies, and rock and roll. *All the Sinners Saints* is a story of people seeking redemption in a world awash in sin.

Loosestrife - Greg Delanty

This book is a chronicle of complicity in our modern lives, a witnessing of war and the destruction of our planet. It is also an attempt to adjust the more destructive blueprint myths of our society. Often our cultural memory tells us to keep quiet about the aspects that are most challenging to our ethics, to forget the violations we feel and tremors that keep us distant and numb.

When You Remember Deir Yassin - R. L. Green

When You Remember Deir Yassin is a collection of poems by R. L. Green, an American Jewish writer, on the subject of the occupation and destruction of Palestine. Green comments: "Outspoken Jewish critics of Israeli crimes against humanity have, strangely, been called 'anti-Semitic' as well as the hilariously illogical epithet 'self-hating Jews.' As a Jewish critic of the Israeli government, I have come to accept these accusations as a stamp of approval and a badge of honor, signifying my own fealty to a central element of Jewish identity and ethics: one must be a lover of truth and a friend to the oppressed, and stand with the victims of tyranny, not with the tyrants, despite tribal loyalty or self-advancement. These poems were written as expressions of outrage, and of grief, and to encourage my sisters and brothers of every cultural or national grouping to speak out against injustice, to try to save Palestine, and in so doing, to reclaim for myself my own place as part of the Jewish people." Poems in the original English are accompanied by Arabic translations.

Roadworthy Creature, Roadworthy Craft - Kate Magill

Words fail but the voice struggles on. The culmination of a decade's worth of performance poetry, *Roadworthy Creature, Roadworthy Craft* is Kate Magill's first full-length publication. In lines that are sinewy yet delicate, Magill's poems explore the terrain where idea and action meet, where bodies and words commingle to form a strange new flesh, a breathing text, an "I" that spirals outward from itself.

Visiting Hours - Jennifer Anne Moses

Visiting Hours, a novel-in-stories, explores the lives of people not normally met on the page—-AIDS patients and those who care for them. Set in Baton Rouge, Louisiana, and written with large and frequent dollops of humor, the book is a profound meditation on faith and love in the face of illness and poverty.

Fomite
Burlington, VT

The Listener Aspires to the Condition of Music - Barry Goldensohn

"I know of no other selected poems that selects on one theme, but this one does, charting Goldensohn's career-long attraction to music's performance, consolations and its august, thrilling, scary and clownish charms. Does all art aspire to the condition of music as Pater claimed, exhaling in a swoon toward that one class act? Goldensohn is more aware than the late 19th century of the overtones of such breathing: his poems thoroughly round out those overtones in a poet's lifetime of listening."
John Peck, poet, editor, Fellow of the American Academy of Rome

The Derivation of Cowboys & Indians - Joseph D. Reich

The Derivation of Cowboys & Indians represents a profound journey, a breakdown of the American Dream from a social, cultural, historical, and spiritual point of view. Reich examines in concise detail the loss of the collective unconscious, commenting on our contemporary postmodern culture with its self-interested excesses, on where and how things all go wrong, and how social/political practice rarely meets its original proclamations and promises. Reich's surreal and self-effacing satire brings this troubling message home. *The Derivation of Cowboys & Indians* is a desperate search and struggle for America's literal, symbolic, and spiritual home.

Views Cost Extra - L.E. Smith

Views that inspire, that calm, or that terrify—all come at some cost to the viewer. In *Views Cost Extra* you will find a New Jersey high school preppy who wants to inhabit the "perfect" cowboy movie, a rural mailman disgusted with the residents of his town who wants to live with the penguins, an ailing screen-writer who strikes a deal with Johnny Cash to reverse an old man's failures, an old man who ponders a young man's suicide attempt, a one-armed blind blues singer who wants to reunite with the car that took her arm on the assembly line— and more. These stories suggest that we must pay something to live even ordinary lives.

Travers' Inferno - L.E. Smith

In the 1970's, churches began to burn in Burlington, Vermont. If it was arson, no one or no reason could be found to blame. This book suggests arson, but makes no claim to historical realism. It claims, instead, to capture the dizzying 70's zeitgeist of aggressive utopian movements, distrust in authority, escapist alternative lifestyles, and a bewildered society of onlookers. In the tradition of John Gardner's *Sunlight Dialogues*, the characters of *Travers' Inferno* are colorful and damaged, sometimes comical, sometimes tragic, looking for meaning through desperate acts. Travers Jones, the protagonist, is grounded in the transcendent—philosophy, epilepsy, arson as purification—and mystified by the opposite sex, haunted by an absent father and directed by an uncle with a grudge. He is seduced by a professor's wife and chased by an endearing if ineffective sergeant of police. There are secessionist Quebecois involved in these church burns who are murdering as well as pilfering and burning. There are changing alliances, violent deaths, lovemaking, and a belligerent cat.

Entanglements - Tony Magistrale

A poet and a painter may employ different mediums to express the same snow-blown afternoon in January, but sometimes they find a way to capture the moment in such a way that their respective visions still manage to stir a reverberation, a connection. In part, that's what *Entanglements* seeks to do. Not so much for the poems and paintings to speak directly to one another, but for them to stir points of similarity.

Fomite
Burlington, VT

The Empty Notebook Interrogates Itself - Susan Thomas

The Empty Notebook began its life as a very literal metaphor for a few weeks of what the poet thought was writer's block, but was really the struggle of an eccentric persona to take over her working life. It won. And for the next three years everything she wrote came to her in the voice of the Empty Notebook, who, as the notebook began to fill itself, became rather opinionated, changed gender, alternately acted as bully and victim, had many bizarre adventures in exotic locales, and developed a somewhat politically incorrect attitude. It then began to steal the voices and forms of other poets and tried to immortalize itself in various poetry reviews. It is now thrilled to collect itself in one slim volume.

My God, What Have We Done? - Susan Weiss

In a world afflicted with war, toxicity, and hunger, does what we do in our private lives really matter? Fifty years after the creation of the atomic bomb at Los Alamos, newlyweds Pauline and Clifford visit that once-secret city on their honeymoon, compelled by Pauline's fascination with Oppenheimer, the soulful scientist. The two stories emerging from this visit reverberate back and forth between the loneliness of a new mother at home in Boston and the isolation of an entire community dedicated to the development of the bomb. While Pauline struggles with unforeseen challenges of family life, Oppenheimer and his crew reckon with forces beyond all imagining. Finally the years of frantic research on the bomb culminate in a stunning test explosion that echoes a rupture in the couple's marriage. Against the backdrop of a civilization that's out of control, Pauline begins to understand the complex, potentially explosive physics of personal relationships. At once funny and dead serious, *My God, What Have We Done?* sifts through the ruins left by the bomb in search of a more worthy human achievement.

As It Is On Earth - Peter M. Wheelwright

Four centuries after the Reformation Pilgrims sailed up the down-flowing watersheds of New England, Taylor Thatcher, irreverent scion of a fallen family of Maine Puritans, is still caught in the turbulence. In his errant attempts to escape from history, the young college professor is further unsettled by his growing attraction to Israeli student Miryam Bluehm as he is swept by Time through the "family thing"—from the tangled genetic and religious history of his New England parents to the redemptive birthday secret of Esther Fleur Noire Bishop, the Cajun-Passamaquoddy woman who raised him and his younger half-cousin/half-brother, Bingham. The landscapes, rivers, and tidal estuaries of Old New England and the Mayan Yucatan are also casualties of history in Thatcher's story of Deep Time and re-discovery of family on Columbus Day at a high-stakes gambling casino, rising in resurrection over the starlit bones of a once-vanquished Pequot Indian tribe.

Love's Labours - Jack Pulaski

In the four stories and two novellas that comprise *Love's Labors* the protagonists, Ben and Laura, discover in their fervid romance and long marriage their interlocking fates, and the histories that preceded their births. They also learned something of the paradox between love and all the things it brings to its beneficiaries: bliss, disaster, duty, tragedy, comedy, the grotesque, and tenderness. Ben and Laura's story is also the particularly American tale of immigration to a new world. Laura's story begins in Puerto Rico, and Ben's lineage is Russian-Jewish. They meet in City College of New York, a place at least analogous to a melting pot. Laura struggles to rescue her brother from gang life and heroin. She is mother to her younger sister; their mother Consuelo is the financial mainstay of the family and consumed by work. Despite filial obligations, Laura aspires to be a serious painter. Ben writes, cares for, and is caught up in the misadventures and surreal stories of his younger schizophrenic brother. Laura is also a story teller as powerful and enchanting as Scheherazade. Ben struggles to survive such riches, and he and Laura endure.

Fomite
Burlington, VT

Suite for Three Voices - *Derek Furr*

Suite for Three Voices is a dance of prose genres, teeming with intense human life in all its humor and sorrow. A son uncovers the horrors of his father's wartime experience, a hitchhiker in a muumuu guards a mysterious parcel, a young man foresees his brother's brush with death on September 11. A Victorian poetess encounters space aliens and digital archives, a runner hears the voice of a dead friend in the song of an indigo bunting, a teacher seeks wisdom from his students' errors and Neil Young. By frozen waterfalls and neglected graveyards, along highways at noon and rivers at dusk, in the sound of bluegrass, Beethoven, and Emily Dickinson, the essays and fiction in this collection offer moments of vision.

The Housing Market - *Joseph D. Reich*

In Joseph Reich's most recent social and cultural, contemporary satire of suburbia entitled, "The Housing market: a comfortable place to jump off the end of the world," the author addresses the absurd, postmodern elements of what it means, or for that matter not, to try and cope and function, and survive and thrive, or live and die in the repetitive and existential, futile and self-destructive, homogenized, monochromatic landscape of a brutal and bland, collective unconscious, which can spiritually result in a gradual wasting away and erosion of the senses or conflict and crisis of a desperate, disproportionate 'situational depression,' triggering and leading the narrator to feel constantly abandoned and stranded, more concretely or proverbially spoken, "the eternal stranger," where when caught between the fight or flight psychological phenomena, naturally repels him and causes him to flee and return without him even knowing it into the wild, while by sudden circumstance and coincidence discovers it surrounds the illusory-like circumference of these selfsame Monopoly board cul-de-sacs and dead ends. Most specifically, what can happen to a solitary, thoughtful, and independent thinker when being stagnated in the triangulation of a cookie-cutter, oppressive culture of a homeowner's association; a memoir all written in critical and didactic, poetic stanzas and passages, and out of desperation, when freedom and control get taken, what he is forced to do in the illusion of 'free will and volition,' something like the derivative art of a smart and ironic and social and cultural satire.

Signed Confessions - *Tom Walker*

Guilt and a desperate need to repent drive the antiheroes in Tom Walker's dark (and often darkly funny) stories: a gullible journalist falls for the 40-year-old stripper he profiles in a magazine, a faithless husband abandons his family and joins a support group for lost souls., a merciless prosecuting attorney grapples with the suicide of his gay son, an aging misanthrope must make amends to five former victims, an egoistic naval hero is haunted by apparitions of his dead wife and a mysterious little girl. The seven tales in *Signed Confessions* measure how far guilty men will go to obtain a forgiveness no one can grant but themselves.

Fomite
Burlington, VT

Still Time - Michael Cocchiarale

Still Time is a collection of twenty-five short and shorter stories exploring tensions that arise in a variety of contemporary relationships: a young boy must deal with the wrath of his out-of-work father; a woman runs into a man twenty years after an awkward sexual encounter; a wife, unable to conceive, imagines her own murder, as well as the reaction of her emotionally distant husband; a soon-to-be-tenured English professor tries to come to terms with her husband's shocking return to the religion of his youth; an assembly line worker, married for thirty years, discovers the surprising secret life of his recently hospitalized wife. Whether a few hundred or a few thousand words, these and other stories in the collection depict characters at moments of deep crisis. Some feel powerless, overwhelmed—unable to do much to change the course of their lives. Others rise to the occasion and, for better or for worse, say or do the thing that might transform them for good. Even in stories with the most troubling of endings, there remains the possibility of redemption. For each of the characters, there is still time.

Raven or Crow - Joshua Amses

Marlowe has recently moved back home to Vermont after flunking his first term at a private college in the Midwest, when his sort-of girlfriend, Eleanor, goes missing. The circumstances surrounding Eleanor's disappearance stand to reveal more about Marlowe than he is willing to allow. Rather than report her missing, he resolves to find Eleanor himself. *Raven or Crow* is the story of mistakes rooted in the ambivalence of being young and without direction.

The Good Muslim of Jackson Heights - Jaysinh Birjépatil

Jackson Heights in this book is a fictional locale with common features assembled from immigrant-friendly neighborhoods around the world where hardworking honest-to-goodness traders from the Indian subcontinent rub shoulders with ruthless entrepreneurs, reclusive antique-dealers, homeless nobodies, merchant-princes, lawyers, doctors, and IT specialists. But as Siraj and Shabnam, urbane newcomers fleeing religious persecution in their homeland, discover, there is no escape from the past. Weaving together the personal and the political. *The Good Muslim of Jackson Heights* is an ambiguous elegy to a utopian ideal set free from all prejudice.

Meanwell - Janice Miller Potter

Meanwell is a twenty-four-poem sequence in which a female servant searches for identity and meaning in the shadow of her mistress, poet Anne Bradstreet. Although Meanwell herself is a fiction, someone like her could easily have existed among Bradstreet's known but unnamed domestic servants. Through Meanwell's eyes, Bradstreet emerges as a human figure during the Great Migration of the 1600s, a period in which the Massachusetts Bay Colony was fraught with physical and political dangers. Through Meanwell, the feelings of women, silenced during the midwife Anne Hutchinson's fiery trial before the Puritan ministers, are finally acknowledged. In effect, the poems are about the making of an American rebel. Through her conflicted conscience, we witness Meanwell's transformation from a powerless English waif to a mythic American who ultimately chooses wilderness over the civilization she has experienced.

Fomite
Burlington, VT

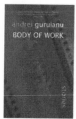

Body of Work - Andrei Guruianu

Throughout thirteen stories, Body of Work chronicles the physical and emotional toll of characters consumed by the all-too-human need for a connection. Their world is achingly common — beauty and regret, obsession and self-doubt, the seductive charm of loneliness. Often fragmented, whimsical, always on the verge of melancholy, the collection is a sepia-toned portrait of nostalgia — each story like an artifact of our impermanence, an embrace of all that we have lost, of all that we might lose and love again someday.

Four-Way Stop - Sherry Olson

If *Thank You* were the only prayer, as Meister Eckhart has suggested, it would be enough, and Sherry Olson's poetry, in her second book, *Four-Way Stop*, would be one. Radical attention, deep love, and dedication to kindness illuminate these poems and the stories she tells us, which are drawn from her own life: with family, with friends, and wherever she travels, with strangers – who to Olson, never are strangers, but kin. Even at the difficult intersections, as in the title poem, *Four-Way Stop,* Olson experiences – and offers – hope, showing us how, *completely unsupervised*, people take turns, with *kindness waving each other on.* Olson writes, knowing that (to quote Czeslaw Milosz) *What surrounds us, here and now, is not guaranteed.* To this world, with her poems, Olson brings – and teaches – attention, generosity, compassion, and appreciative joy. —Carol Henrikson

Dons of Time - Greg Guma

"Wherever you look...there you are." The next media breakthrough has just happened. They call it Remote Viewing and Tonio Wolfe is at the center of the storm. But the research underway at TELPORT's off-the-books lab is even more radical -- opening a window not only to remote places but completely different times. Now unsolved mysteries are colliding with cutting edge science and altered states of consciousness in a world of corporate gangsters, infamous crimes and top-secret experiments. Based on eyewitness accounts, suppressed documents and the lives of world-changers like Nikola Tesla, Annie Besant and Jack the Ripper, Dons of Time is a speculative adventure, a glimpse of an alternative future and a quantum leap to Gilded Age London at the tipping point of invention, revolution and murder.

Screwed – Stephen Goldberg

Screwed is a collection of five plays by Stephen Goldberg, who has written over twenty-five produced plays and is co-founder of the Off Center or the Dramatic Arts in Burlington, Vermont.

My Father's Keeper - Andrew Potok

The turmoil, terror and betrayal of their escape from Poland at the start of World War II lead us into this tale of hatred and forgiveness between father and son.

Fomite
Burlington, VT

Alfabestiario
AlphaBetaBestiario - Antonello Borra

Animals have always understood that mankind is not fully at home in the world. Bestiaries, hoping to teach, send out warnings. This one, of course, aims at doing the same.

The Consequence of Gesture - L.E. Smith

On a Monday evening in December of 1980, Mark David Chapman murdered John Lennon outside his apartment building in New York City. The Consequence of Gesture brings the reader along a three-day countdown to mayhem. This book inserts Chapman into the weekend plans of a group of friends sympathetic with his obsession to shatter a cultural icon and determined to perform their own iconoclastic gestures. John Lennon's life is not the only one that hangs in the balance. No one will emerge the same.

Sinfonia Bulgarica—Zdravka Evtimova

Sinfonia Bulgarica is a novel about four women in contemporary Bulgaria: a rich cold-blooded heiress, a masseuse dreaming of peace and quiet that never come, a powerful wife of the most influential man in the country, and a waitress struggling against all odds to win a victory over lies, poverty and humiliation. It is a realistic book of vice and yearning, of truthfulness and schemes, of love and desperation. The heroes are plain-spoken characters, whose action is limited by the contradictions of a society where lowness rules at many levels. The novel draws a picture of life in a country where many people believe that "Money is the most loyal friend of man". Yet the four women have an even more loyal friend: ruthlessness of life.

Unfinished Stories of Girls—Catherine Zobal Dent

The sixteen stories in this debut collection set on the Eastern Shore of Maryland feature powerfully drawn characters with troubles and subjects such as communal guilt over a drunk-driving car accident that kills a young girl, the doomed marriage of a jewelry clerk and an undercover cop, the obsessions of a housecleaner jailed for forging her employers' signatures, the heart-breaking closeness of a family stuck in the snow. Each of Unfinished Stories of Girls' richly textured tales is embedded in the quiet and sometimes violent fields, towns, and riverbeds that are the backdrop for life in tidewater Maryland. Dent's deep love for her region shines through, but so does her melancholic thoughtfulness about its challenges and problems. The reader is invited inside the lives of characters trying to figure out the marshy world around them, when that world leaves much up to the imagination

Writing a review on Amazon, Good Reads, Shelfari, Library Thing or other social media sites for readers will help the progress of independent publishing. To submit a review, go to the book page on any of the sites and follow the links for reviews. Books from independent presses rely on reader to reader communications.

Made in the USA
Middletown, DE
18 January 2019